Mr.CEO and Miss.Clumsy

His Imperfect Wife

Bhoomi Reddy

Contents

Chapter I

The Marraige Proposal

The sun dipped low over Mumbai, casting a golden hue across the bustling streets. Car horns blared in a cacophony of urban life, a symphony of chaos that matched the rhythm of the city's heartbeat. Amidst the clamor, Ammu stood in her childhood bedroom, surrounded by posters of dreamy actors and scattered drawings of her ideal life. Her twin sister, Priya, sat cross-legged on the bed, scrolling through her phone with an unimpressed expression.

"Do you think he'll be tall? Like, tall enough to reach the top shelf?" Ammu mused, twirling a strand of her unruly hair around her finger.

Priya glanced up, raising an eyebrow. "Ammu, you're marrying him in a week. Shouldn't you be thinking about, I don't know, the marriage part?"

"The marriage part is boring!" Ammu giggled, bouncing on her toes. "I want to know if he'll sweep me off my feet! Oh, and what if he knows how to cook? That would be amazing!"

"Or what if he doesn't?" Priya deadpanned. "You might be the one sweeping him off his feet if he can't boil water."

Ammu laughed, a light, melodic sound that filled the room. "Stop! What if he's like one of those romantic heroes who serenades me under the stars?" She clasped her hands together, her eyes sparkling with excitement. "Maybe he'll have a guitar and everything!"

"Right, because that's what every CEO does after a long day of meetings—strums the guitar to his new wife," Priya snorted, flipping her hair back. "Let me guess, he'll also have a pet dog named Max?"

"Of course!" Ammu declared, her voice rising with enthusiasm. "Max will be my little sidekick, and we'll go on adventures together!"

Priya rolled her eyes but couldn't hide her smile. "You're impossible, you know that?"

"Impossibly hopeful!" Ammu shot back, grinning widely. "I just want a husband who's kind and fun. Is that too much to ask?"

Meanwhile, across the city in a sleek high-rise office overlooking the Arabian Sea, Arhan sat at his imposing mahogany desk, staring at the portfolio spread before him. The weight of his father's expectations loomed over him like the skyscrapers outside his window. He drummed his fingers impatiently, each tap echoing like a countdown in his mind.

"Arhan," Kethan, his younger brother and personal secretary, said as he entered the room with a clipboard in hand. "Your parents are on the line again. They're really pushing for this marriage."

Arhan frowned, leaning back in his chair. "I know, Kethan. But I'm not ready to settle down. I've got a company to run, and I don't need distractions."

"Except they're not exactly giving you a choice." Kethan sighed, sliding a document across the desk. "They want to meet Ammu's family tomorrow. You might want to consider at least pretending to be interested."

"Pretending is all I can do," Arhan muttered, glancing at the photos of the young woman he was supposed to marry. "She's just a girl. What's the big deal?"

"An arranged marriage is a big deal to your parents," Kethan reminded him, his tone firm yet sympathetic. "They think it's time for you to settle down and start a family."

"Tell them I'm busy." Arhan waved his hand dismissively, but the weight of responsibility settled heavily on his shoulders.

"Busy doing what? Staring at spreadsheets? You're going to have to face this sooner or later," Kethan replied, crossing his arms.

"Fine! I'll meet her, but that doesn't mean I'll fall in love." Arhan's voice was resolute, but deep down, a tiny flicker of curiosity ignited. What was Ammu really like?

Back in her bedroom, Ammu was still lost in her daydreams, her imagination painting a picture of a love story that felt like it had leapt from the pages of a novel.

"What if he has a dark secret?" Ammu said suddenly, her eyes wide with intrigue.

"Like what? That he's really a spy?" Priya quipped, the corners of her mouth twitching.

"Yes! Or maybe he's a prince in disguise!" Ammu exclaimed, bouncing off her bed. "Oh, I can see it now—"

"Or maybe he's just a guy who wants to run his father's company," Priya interrupted, shaking her head. "Ammu, you need to be realistic."

"Realistic is overrated," Ammu retorted, her voice light as she twirled around the room. "I want magic! I want adventure! What if he takes me to Paris? Or a beach in Bali?"

Priya laughed, shaking her head. "You do realize you're marrying him for a reason, right? It's not a vacation package."

"Details, details," Ammu waved her sister off, her heart brimming with anticipation. "I just hope he's not a complete bore."

"Or a jerk," Priya added, the seriousness creeping into her voice. "You deserve someone who treats you well, Ammu."

"I know, I know!" Ammu said, her expression softening. "But what if he's just misunderstood? Like in the movies?"

Priya shot her a skeptical look. "Movies aren't real life, Ammu."

"Maybe not, but love is!" Ammu said, beaming. "And I'm going to make it work!"

As the night deepened, Arhan found himself staring out at the city skyline, the twinkling lights mirroring the stars above. He thought of his parents and their relentless push for tradition, for stability.

"Are you really going to do this?" Nishan's voice broke through his thoughts as he sauntered into the office, a mischievous grin plastered on his face. "I can't believe you're actually going through with an arranged marriage."

"Believe it," Arhan replied, his tone flat. "I'm doing it for my parents."

Nishan chuckled, leaning against the doorframe. "And what if she turns out to be a complete disaster? You know how clumsy girls can be."

"Clumsy?" Arhan frowned, remembering the photos he had seen of Ammu. "I don't want a disaster. I want someone who can keep up."

"Keep up with what? Your endless meetings? Your 'CEO' lifestyle?" Nishan laughed. "You need someone who can lighten up your world, not fit into your corporate box."

"Look, I'm not looking for a partner in crime. I need someone who can handle their own," Arhan snapped, but a part of him wondered if that was really true.

Nishan tilted his head, a knowing glint in his eye. "You say that now, but wait until you meet her. You might find she's not what you expect."

"Or she might be exactly what I expect—a distraction." Arhan leaned back in his chair, crossing his arms.

"Just don't ignore the possibility of a magic spark," Nishan said with a wink before leaving, leaving Arhan alone with his thoughts and the distant sounds of the city.

As he turned back to his desk, he found himself staring at the stack of documents again, but his mind drifted back to Ammu. The girl he had seen in fleeting photos had a bright smile, an infectious laugh. What if she was the one who could break through his cold exterior?

Ammu lay in bed that night, staring at the ceiling, her heart racing with anticipation. She envisioned her future husband—tall, charming, and with a hidden romantic side. "He'll be perfect," she whispered to herself, her voice filled with hope.

"Or he might just be a guy who eats cereal for dinner," Priya commented from her own bed, snickering softly.

Ammu rolled her eyes, a grin spreading on her lips. "I'll still love him, even if he's a cereal guy!"

The night wore on, filled with dreams of love and laughter, both Ammu and Arhan unaware of the journey that awaited them. They were two strangers on the brink of something extraordinary, each holding a piece of the other's heart, waiting for the moment it would all click into place.

As the dawn broke over Mumbai, a new day began, filled with the promise of adventure, laughter, and perhaps, just perhaps, love.

Chapter 2

A Futile Meet

Ammu stood in front of her mirror, admiring the reflection that gazed back at her. The soft, pastel-colored dress hugged her curves in all the right places, while her hair cascaded in playful waves around her shoulders. A few stray strands danced across her forehead, but she simply tucked them behind her ear with a smile. "Today's the day!" she chirped, twirling in front of the mirror.

Her heart raced with excitement as she imagined how the day would unfold. "He's going to be so charming and handsome," she whispered to herself, her cheeks flushing at the thought. With a giddy laugh, she grabbed her phone and dialed Ananya's number, practically bouncing on her toes as she waited for her friend to pick up.

"Heyyy!" Ananya's voice burst through the speaker, filled with enthusiasm. "Are you ready for the big moment?"

"Ready? I'm practically vibrating!" Ammu exclaimed, her eyes sparkling. "I've picked out the perfect dress, and I'm feeling like a princess! Can you believe I'm about to meet my husband?"

"Wait, wait," Ananya interrupted, laughter bubbling in her voice. "Did you just say husband? It hasn't even happened yet!"

"Positive thinking!" Ammu replied, giggling. "I can picture it now—Arhan will see me, and he'll be so blown away by my beauty that he'll—"

"—fall to his knees and propose on the spot?" Ananya teased, cutting her off.

"Exactly!" Ammu squealed, her imagination running wild. "And then we'll ride off into the sunset together!"

"Alright, alright, just remember to breathe," Ananya chuckled. "And if he doesn't fall to his knees, I will!"

"Deal! And just to be safe, I'm going to video call Vihaan," Ammu said, her fingers already tapping on her phone.

"Good idea! He'll be your cheerleader," Ananya replied, her voice brimming with energy.

Vihaan answered almost immediately, his face lighting up the screen. "Ammu! You look incredible! What's the plan?"

"I'm meeting Arhan today!" Ammu announced, her excitement spilling over. "I'm all dressed up and ready to impress."

"Wow, look at you! You're going to knock him off his feet," Vihaan said, his eyes sparkling with admiration. "But hey, don't forget to be yourself. He needs to see the real Ammu."

"Of course! I'm just a bit nervous," she admitted, twirling a lock of hair around her finger. "What if he doesn't like me?"

"Impossible!" Ananya chimed in, waving her hands dramatically. "You're the most charming person I know. If he can't see that, he's blind!"

"True, true!" Ammu laughed, feeling the warmth of her friends' encouragement wash over her. "Okay, I'm going to show him just how amazing I am!"

"Just don't trip on your way to him!" Vihaan joked, and they all laughed, the sound echoing through the phone.

"I'll try my best!" Ammu said through giggles, her heart still fluttering with anticipation. "I'll call you both after the meeting!"

"Can't wait to hear every detail!" Ananya said, her voice a mix of excitement and teasing. "And remember, make eye contact!"

"Right! Eye contact, got it!" Ammu nodded, her determination shining through.

As she hung up, her thoughts danced around the romantic possibilities. Would he take her to a fancy restaurant? Maybe they'd stroll by the beach or share stories over coffee. With a sigh of blissful anticipation, she grabbed her purse and headed out, her heart humming with hope.

The ride to the café felt like an eternity. Ammu gazed out at the bustling streets of Mumbai, where life thrived in every corner. The aroma of street food wafted through the air, mixed with the sounds of laughter and chatter. She couldn't help but smile, envisioning her future with Arhan.

But as she stepped into the café, her heart sank. The place was buzzing with energy, but there was no sign of Arhan. She checked her phone, tapping her foot nervously. "Maybe he's just running late," she reassured herself, scanning the room, her heart still hopeful.

Minutes turned into what felt like hours. Ammu fiddled with her phone, trying to distract herself, but the steady tick of the clock felt louder than the chatter around her. With each passing moment, her excitement began to wane, replaced by a creeping sense of disappointment.

Just as she was about to text her friends for support, her phone buzzed. It was a message from Kethan, Arhan's brother.

"Sorry, Ammu. Arhan won't be able to make it today. He got caught up in a business meeting. We'll reschedule soon."

Ammu's heart dropped. "What?" she whispered, her voice barely audible over the café's noise. "He's not coming?" The words hung in the air, heavy and disheartening.

"Are you okay?" Ammu murmured to herself, her heart pounding in a way that felt more like betrayal than disappointment. She had dreamt of this moment, and now it was slipping away like sand through her fingers.

Determined to keep her spirits up, she took a deep breath and texted her friends.

"Hey, change of plans. Arhan isn't coming. He has a meeting."

Ananya responded immediately, her concern palpable even through the screen. "What? No! I'm so sorry, Ammu. Do you want us to come over?"

"Yeah, I think I need some cheering up." Ammu sighed, staring out at the busy streets, feeling utterly deflated.

As she sat alone at the table, the café felt more isolating than before. The laughter around her seemed like a mocking reminder of her own loneliness. She absentmindedly stirred her drink, watching the ice clink against the glass.

When her phone buzzed again, it was Vihaan. "I'm really sorry, Ammu. I thought you'd finally get to meet him. Do you want me to come over?"

"No, it's okay. I'll be fine," she replied, trying to muster a smile. "I just thought... well, I pictured it differently."

"Just remember, this isn't the end," he texted back. "You'll get another chance. He's probably just busy being a 'CEO' or whatever."

"Yeah, a CEO who doesn't care about spending time with his future wife," Ammu mumbled, staring at her drink.

"Hey, don't be like that," Vihaan replied. "You deserve someone who'll prioritize you. Maybe it's a sign that he's not worth your time."

Ammu rolled her eyes at her phone. "You sound just like Priya. Maybe you're right, but I just wanted to give him a chance. I wanted to see if there was a spark."

"Then there will be, just not today," Vihaan assured her. "Let's plan a day for a girls' night. I'll bring snacks and we'll binge-watch rom-coms. They always help."

Ammu couldn't help but smile at the thought. "That sounds perfect. I need a good dose of cheesy love stories."

"See? You'll get through this!" Vihaan replied with a string of cheerful emojis.

As the café began to empty, Ammu finally decided to leave. She stepped out into the bustling streets of Mumbai, the warmth of the sun hitting her face. The reality of the day was not how she had envisioned it. Her heart felt heavier, filled with uncertainty about her future with Arhan.

Ammu walked slowly, letting the vibrant energy of the city wash over her, but her mind kept wandering back to Arhan. What was he like? Would he ever be the kind of husband she dreamed of?

Later that evening, she lay on her bed, staring at the ceiling, replaying the day in her mind. "What if he's not into this marriage?" she murmured, the thought sending a shiver down her spine.

Priya poked her head in, a concerned look on her face. "Hey, how did it go?"

Ammu sighed, turning to face her sister. "He didn't show up. He had a meeting."

"Oh, Ammu," Priya said softly, sitting next to her. "I'm so sorry."

"I was so excited," Ammu admitted, the disappointment threatening to spill over. "I thought maybe… maybe he'd be different. Maybe he'd see me and realize how perfect we'd be together."

Priya wrapped an arm around her. "You're perfect just the way you are, Ammu. If he can't see that, it's his loss."

"But what if he's just busy? What if he has a lot on his plate?" Ammu countered, her voice barely above a whisper.

"Or maybe he's just not ready for this," Priya said, her tone gentle but firm. "You deserve someone who wants to be with you, not someone who makes excuses."

Ammu nodded, feeling the weight of her sister's words settle deep within her. "I know." She took a deep breath, trying to shake off the lingering disappointment. "I guess I'll just have to wait and see."

With a sigh, Ammu sat up, her thoughts swirling. "Maybe I'll give it another shot. Maybe he'll surprise me next time."

"Exactly! And in the meantime, let's focus on you. We can plan something fun!" Priya suggested, her eyes glimmering with mischief.

"Like what?" Ammu asked, a small smile creeping onto her face.

"Like a makeover! You'll be the belle of the ball next time you see him," Priya declared, her excitement infectious.

Ammu laughed, feeling the heaviness in her heart lift just a little. "Alright, let's do it! But I'm not changing who I am."

"Never!" Priya agreed, squeezing her sister's shoulder. "Just enhancing the fabulousness!"

As the evening wore on, the sisters plotted and planned, Ammu's heart still hopeful, still dreaming of the day when she and Arhan would finally meet face to face—not just as strangers but as partners in a love story waiting to unfold.

Chapter 3

The Meet

The sun dipped low in the Mumbai skyline, casting a warm, golden hue over Ammu's house. The buzz of excitement filled the air as her family prepared for the engagement ceremony the next day. Her heart raced with anticipation, thoughts of Arhan swirling in her mind. "This is it, Ammu," she whispered to herself, smoothing down the dress she had chosen for the occasion.

"Ammu! Are you ready?" Ananya called from the living room, her voice a mixture of eagerness and mischief.

"Almost!" Ammu replied, darting one last look in the mirror. She wanted to make a good impression, and she hoped that her clumsiness wouldn't show. She took a deep breath, the sweet scent of jasmine from the flowers decorating the room filling her lungs.

As she stepped into the living room, her mother, Swetha, was fussing over the arrangements. "Ammu, sweetheart, remember to be on your best behavior when Arhan's family arrives. We want to make a good impression," she instructed, a hint of urgency in her voice.

"I will, Mom! I promise," Ammu said, her voice bubbling with excitement. "But what if I trip or say something silly?"

"Just be yourself," her sister Priya chimed in, her tone calm and collected. "That's good enough."

Ammu nodded, grateful for her sister's reassurance. Just then, the doorbell rang, and her heart leaped. "He's here!" she squealed, her eyes widening.

"Stay calm!" Priya said, a teasing smile on her face.

Ammu took a deep breath, trying to steady her racing heart. As she opened the door, her breath caught in her throat. There stood Arhan, tall and impeccably dressed, his presence commanding yet unexpectedly warm. The sunlight framed his features, making him look even more dashing.

"Hello, Ammu," he said, his voice deep and confident.

"Hi, Arhan," she managed to reply, her cheeks flushing as she stepped aside to let him in.

As he entered, Ammu couldn't help but notice the way his eyes scanned the room, taking in the vibrant colors and decorations. "Wow, your house looks beautiful," he commented, a hint of admiration in his voice.

"Thank you! We wanted everything to be perfect for tomorrow," she said, trying to sound more mature than she felt.

Kethan, Arhan's brother, followed closely behind, his eyes gleaming with mischief. "And I think you both look perfect too," he added, a playful smirk on his lips. "You must be Ammu."

"I am!" she replied, trying to suppress her nervousness.

"Lucky guy, huh?" Kethan winked at Arhan, who simply nodded, a slight smile playing on his lips.

As they settled in the living room, Ammu felt a flutter in her stomach. The atmosphere was filled with laughter and light banter as her family mingled with Arhan's. She overheard Kethan say to Arhan, "You've got a gem here, brother. She's stunning."

"Yeah, I know," Arhan said, his gaze momentarily locking onto Ammu, who was trying to act nonchalant as she poured some juice. "I'm lucky."

Ammu's heart raced as she caught his eye, a shy smile breaking across her face. Kethan's attention shifted, and he glanced over at Priya, who was standing by the window, her arms crossed, observing the dynamics in the room. "And who's this?" he asked, clearly intrigued.

"That's my sister Priya," Ammu introduced, a hint of pride in her voice.

"Nice to meet you, Priya," Kethan said, his tone smooth. "You've got to be the responsible one, huh? Keeping this one in check?" He gestured toward Ammu, who was now blushing furiously.

Priya raised an eyebrow, her expression cool and composed. "I try my best," she replied, a faint smile touching her lips.

"You should let loose a bit. Life's too short to be serious all the time," Kethan suggested, his charm evident.

"I'll keep that in mind," Priya said, her tone polite yet firm, turning her attention back to the conversation in the room, leaving Kethan momentarily baffled.

Meanwhile, Ammu felt a mix of excitement and anxiety. She wanted to impress Arhan, but her clumsiness often got the best of her. As she tried to balance a tray of snacks, her hand slipped, sending a plate of samosas tumbling to the floor with a loud thud.

"Oh no!" she gasped, her face burning with embarrassment.

Arhan quickly knelt down to help her. "It's alright. No harm done," he said, his eyes softening as he picked up the pieces.

"Sorry, I'm so clumsy," Ammu mumbled, her cheeks flushed.

"I think it's endearing," he replied, a teasing smile on his face.

"Endearing?" Kethan chimed in, grinning. "That's one way to put it. I'd say it's a sign of excitement!"

"Shut up, Kethan!" Ammu shot back, unable to hide her laughter at the absurdity of the situation.

As the evening unfolded, the conversation flowed easily. They discussed the wedding plans, and Ammu felt her nervousness ebb as she got to know Arhan better. He was surprisingly down-to-earth, and his laughter was contagious.

"Tomorrow's going to be amazing!" Ammu declared, her excitement bubbling over.

"Definitely," Arhan agreed, a glimmer of sincerity in his eyes. "I'm looking forward to it."

Kethan leaned back, observing the budding chemistry between his brother and Ammu. "You two look good together. Just don't let her trip over her own feet at the engagement," he teased, earning a playful swat from Ammu.

"I'll do my best," Arhan replied, a chuckle escaping his lips.

As the night wore on, Ammu felt a warmth spreading in her chest. She watched Arhan interact with her family, his charm effortlessly winning them over. "He's really not what I expected," she thought, a smile creeping onto her face.

"Hey, Ammu," Kethan called out, leaning closer. "What do you think of my brother? Be honest."

Ammu glanced at Arhan, who was now deep in conversation with her father. "He's... charming, I guess," she replied, her heart skipping a beat.

"Charming? Is that all?" Kethan teased, raising an eyebrow. "You should be gushing! He's a CEO, you know!"

"I'm not that easily impressed," she said, feigning indifference.

"Right, right," Kethan laughed. "But seriously, you're a lucky girl. Just don't let him intimidate you."

"Intimidate me?" Ammu scoffed, though she felt a flutter of nerves at the thought. "He's not intimidating. He's just... tall."

"Tall and handsome," Kethan added, winking at her.

Just then, Arhan turned to them. "What are you two plotting?" he asked, a smirk on his face.

"Just discussing how lucky Ammu is," Kethan said with a grin.

"Lucky indeed," Arhan replied, his gaze softening as he looked at Ammu. "I think I'm the lucky one. You have a wonderful family."

"Thanks!" Ammu beamed, her heart swelling with pride.

As the evening continued, Ammu felt more at ease. She and Arhan exchanged stories, laughter echoing through the room. She discovered his passion for business and his love for adventure. "I've always wanted to go skydiving," Ammu confessed, her eyes wide with excitement.

"Skydiving?" Arhan raised an eyebrow, clearly intrigued. "That sounds... exhilarating."

"Or terrifying!" Kethan chimed in, shaking his head. "You'd have to convince me to jump out of a plane."

Ammu laughed, "It's all about the thrill! You should try it."

As the night drew to a close, Ammu found herself wishing it wouldn't end. "Can we do this again?" she blurted out, her heart racing at her audacity.

"Absolutely," Arhan replied, a genuine smile on his face. "I'd love to."

As they all gathered to say their goodbyes, Ammu felt a wave of warmth envelop her. "Tomorrow's going to be special," she thought, her heart humming with hope.

Kethan nudged Arhan playfully. "You better not mess this up, brother. You've got a catch."

"I won't," Arhan assured him, his gaze lingering on Ammu.

As Arhan and Kethan left, Ammu stood at the door, her heart fluttering with happiness. "He really is something," she mused, her cheeks still warm from their earlier laughter.

"See? That wasn't so difficult, was it?" Priya asked, a knowing smile on her face as she joined her sister at the door.

"No, it was... amazing," Ammu replied, her eyes shining with excitement.

"Just remember to be yourself tomorrow," Priya advised, her tone serious yet supportive. "He's marrying you, not a facade."

"I will," Ammu promised, her heart steadying. "I just hope I don't trip again."

Priya laughed, shaking her head. "You'll be fine. Just enjoy every moment."

As Ammu prepared for bed that night, her mind raced with thoughts of Arhan. "Tomorrow is going to be perfect," she whispered to herself, her heart full of hope for what was to come.

Chapter 4

His Thoughts

The streets of Mumbai buzzed with the usual evening chaos as Arhan and Kethan stepped into the plush confines of their car. The weight of the day hung heavily on Arhan's shoulders. He leaned back against the seat, staring out the window at the passing lights, their flickering reflections dancing across his troubled expression.

"What's with the long face?" Kethan asked, breaking the silence. He turned towards Arhan, a teasing grin plastered on his features. "Did you realize you're stuck in an arranged marriage with a clumsy girl?"

Arhan shot him a glance, irritation flickering in his eyes. "It's not just that, Kethan. It's... complicated." He sighed, rubbing the back of his neck. "I mean, what if I can't adjust to her?"

"Adjust?" Kethan raised an eyebrow, amusement dancing in his voice. "What's wrong with her? You saw her today. She's sweet, bubbly, and all things nice! You think she's messy, but that's just her charm. Besides, it's not like you're some prince charming yourself."

Arhan turned to face his brother, annoyance bubbling up. "You don't get it. She's not the polished type. She's... clumsy." He shook his head, recalling the way Ammu had tripped over her own feet while serving snacks, the samosas falling in a dramatic cascade. "She's too carefree, and I'm not sure I can deal with that."

"Carefree?" Kethan chuckled, shaking his head. "Man, you're really overthinking this. Who needs a perfect partner when you've got someone who can make you laugh? And that's exactly what she did, didn't she?"

Arhan stared out the window, his thoughts tangled in uncertainty. "I pretended to be happy today. You know, for our parents. They've been pushing this marriage since forever." His voice dropped a notch, the weight of responsibility evident. "I don't want to disappoint them."

Kethan leaned back, his expression turning serious. "You're not just marrying for your parents, Arhan. You're marrying for yourself too. If you go into this with a mindset that she won't be perfect, you'll never see the good in her." He paused, gauging his brother's reaction. "What is it that really worries you?"

"What if I can't handle her? She's so different from... from what I imagined." Arhan ran a hand through his hair, frustration boiling beneath the surface. "I've always been the one in control. I can't just let loose and be... goofy. That's not me."

Kethan smirked, leaning forward as if he were about to unveil the greatest secret. "Maybe it's time to let go of all that. You work too hard, and you take life too seriously. Ammu could be the spark you didn't know you needed."

"I don't want a spark; I want stability." Arhan's voice was firm, yet uncertainty lingered in his eyes. "She looks a little messy, and I just... I'm not sure I can adapt to that."

"Messy?" Kethan laughed, shaking his head in disbelief. "Dude, she's like a breath of fresh air. You're used to your corporate world where everything is structured and planned. But life isn't a board meeting. It's chaotic, unpredictable, and that's what makes it beautiful. Ammu is what you need."

Arhan sighed deeply, his gaze drifting back to the city lights. "You make it sound so easy. But what if I fail? What if I can't make her happy? What if she expects me to be someone I'm not?"

"Listen, it's not about being someone you're not. Just be yourself! She's not expecting a fairy tale. She just wants you to be there, to be real." Kethan nudged Arhan's shoulder playfully, trying to lighten the mood. "Besides, if you're really that worried, just ask her about her past. You might discover something that'll change your perspective."

Arhan turned to Kethan, a hint of curiosity breaking through his cloud of doubt. "You really think it's worth it?"

"I know it is. And if she trips over her own feet again, at least you'll have a good laugh. That's way better than a perfect partner with no personality." Kethan's grin was infectious, making Arhan crack a reluctant smile.

"Maybe you're right," Arhan conceded, though uncertainty still clung to him like a shadow.

"Of course I am! Now, let's go home and get some sleep. You've got a wedding to prepare for, and you don't want to be all grumpy on your big day, do you?"

Arhan chuckled softly, the weight on his chest easing slightly. "No, I suppose I don't."

As they pulled into the driveway, Arhan's thoughts spiraled back to Ammu. Her laughter, the way she lit up the room with her energy, and that infectious smile danced in his mind. Despite his reservations, a flicker of hope began to ignite within him.

"Hey, Arhan?" Kethan called, pausing as he stepped out of the car. "Just remember, it's about the journey, not the destination. You might be surprised where it takes you."

Arhan nodded, watching as Kethan disappeared into the house. He lingered for a moment, staring at the starry sky above, contemplating the whirlwind of emotions swirling within him. "What if I actually enjoy being with her?" he mused, the thought both thrilling and terrifying.

Later that night, as he lay in bed, Arhan's mind was a flurry of thoughts. Ammu's clumsiness, her bright laughter, and the warmth of her presence filled his mind. "Maybe I am being too hard on her," he whispered to himself, the faint sound echoing in the stillness of the room. "Maybe she really is the person I need."

With a sigh, he turned off the light, plunging the room into darkness. As sleep began to take him, the uncertainty lingered, but so did a newfound curiosity. Tomorrow would be a new day, and perhaps it was time to embrace this chaos called love.

Chapter 5

The Engagement Day

The sun dipped low in the sky, casting a warm golden glow over the bustling streets of Mumbai. The air was thick with excitement, a palpable energy that seemed to hum through the crowd. Today was Arhan and Ammu's engagement day, and the grand hall was filled with laughter, chatter, and the clinking of glasses.

Kethan adjusted his tie, surveying the elegantly decorated venue. "Wow, this place looks like it was lifted straight from a fairy tale," he said, glancing around. His attention landed on Priya, Ammu's twin sister, who glided through the room in a stunning emerald dress, her hair cascading down her shoulders like a waterfall.

"Hey there, princess!" Kethan called out, flashing his most charming grin. "You're glowing tonight. Did you steal the spotlight from the sun?"

Priya raised an eyebrow, her lips curling into a smirk. "Flattery won't get you anywhere, Kethan. I'm not some easy target you can charm with your smooth talk."

Kethan chuckled, undeterred. "You're right. I'm just hoping you'll at least consider me for a dance later."

"Keep dreaming," she shot back, her voice laced with playful sarcasm as she walked away, leaving Kethan with a chuckle and a shake of his head.

As the guests mingled, Ananya arrived, her laughter ringing out like music. She spotted Kethan and waved him over. "What are you doing, trying to flirt with Priya? She's not your type, you know that!"

"Who says?" Kethan protested, rolling his eyes. "She might just need a little convincing. I mean, look at her! She's gorgeous."

"Or she might just need someone who knows how to take a hint," Ananya retorted, her eyes sparkling with mischief. "Besides, I'm pretty sure she's more into her studies than into you."

Kethan pouted. "You're ruining my chances here, Ananya. But tell me, where's Ammu? I was hoping to get a glimpse of the bride-to-be."

"Patience, my dear Kethan. She'll be here soon," Ananya replied, scanning the room. "Vihaan's already on the lookout for her."

Vihaan stood at the edge of the hall, his eyes glued to the entrance, anticipation etched on his face. His crush on Ammu was no secret, but he'd never found the courage to confess his feelings. Instead, he watched her from afar, a bittersweet smile tugging at his lips.

"Come on, Ammu. Where are you?" he murmured under his breath, frustration creeping in. Just then, Arhan entered the room, his presence commanding attention. He wore a tailored suit that accentuated his sharp features, but his eyes were distant, as if he were somewhere else entirely.

Kethan nudged Arhan playfully. "You know, you might want to smile at least. People are starting to wonder if you're here for a funeral."

Arhan shot him a sideways glance, his expression unchanging. "I'm not here to entertain them," he replied coolly, adjusting his cufflinks with a sigh.

"Maybe not, but they're here to celebrate you and Ammu," Kethan pressed, trying to lighten the mood. "A little warmth wouldn't hurt."

Arhan shifted his gaze back to the entrance, his mind racing. "I'm not interested in this whole charade. I'm doing this for my parents."

"Sure, but you might want to at least look like you care," Kethan advised, his tone half-joking but with a hint of sincerity.

Before Arhan could respond, Ammu entered the hall like a ray of sunshine, her vibrant dress flowing as she moved. The room fell silent, all eyes on her. Her smile lit up the space, and for a moment, time stood still. Arhan's breath caught in his throat, and the world around him faded away.

"Wow," Kethan whispered, nudging Arhan again. "Look at her. She's like a princess."

Arhan blinked, momentarily entranced. "She looks… different," he muttered, shaking himself out of the daze. "But it doesn't matter. This is just a formality."

Vihaan, standing nearby, couldn't take his eyes off Ammu. Regret washed over him, gnawing at his insides. What if he'd confessed his feelings earlier? Would things have been different? His heart ached as he watched her laugh, completely unaware of the turmoil in his chest.

"Look at her," he whispered to himself, frustration mingling with longing. "How could I have let her slip away?"

Nishan, ever the charmer, noticed Ananya standing off to the side, a playful grin spreading across his face. "Well, well, if it isn't the most beautiful woman in the room," he said, striding over with confidence. "Care for a dance, or should I just stand here and admire you from afar?"

Ananya rolled her eyes but couldn't suppress a smile. "You really think you can charm me with your usual lines, don't you?"

"Of course! But let's be honest, it's not just the lines. It's the whole package," Nishan replied with a wink, his playful demeanor making Ananya laugh.

"Nice try, but I'm not falling for your tricks today," she countered, her eyes sparkling with amusement. "I'm here to support Ammu, not get swept away by some playboy."

As the music began to play, Ammu laughed, spinning around, her joy infectious. "Can you believe it? We're really doing this!" she exclaimed to the gathered guests, her voice ringing with excitement.

Arhan watched her, a mix of admiration and confusion swirling within him. Why couldn't he shake the feeling that there was more to her than just clumsiness? Her innocence was captivating, and for a fleeting moment, he felt a tug at his heart.

Kethan leaned in closer to Arhan, breaking his reverie. "See? That's what I'm talking about. She's not just a clumsy girl. She's full of life!"

Arhan sighed, running a hand through his hair. "I know, but... it's complicated," he admitted, his voice low. "I'm not sure I can handle all this."

"Then figure it out!" Kethan insisted, his tone shifting to one of seriousness. "You're marrying her, man. You can't just stand there looking like a statue."

The guests began to mingle again, and Vihaan took a step forward, his heart racing. This was his chance. He approached Ammu, trying to gather his thoughts. "Ammu, you look… um, stunning," he stammered, his nerves getting the better of him.

"Thanks, Vihaan!" she replied, her eyes sparkling with joy. "I can't believe it's finally happening. I'm so excited!"

"Yeah, me too," he said, forcing a smile. "So, um, how do you feel about everything?"

Ammu shrugged, her expression playful. "I feel like I'm in a dream! But it's also a little scary, don't you think?"

"Scary?" Vihaan echoed, his heart sinking a bit. "You mean… you're nervous?"

"Not really nervous, just… you know, a little overwhelmed," she admitted, twirling a strand of hair around her finger. "But I have high hopes for this! I want to make it work."

Vihaan swallowed hard, wishing he could tell her how he felt. "You'll do great. I mean, you're amazing, Ammu. Anyone would be lucky to have you."

Her eyes lit up at his words, but before he could muster the courage to say more, Arhan approached, his expression unreadable. "Ammu, we should… um, greet the guests," he said, his tone flat.

"Of course!" she chirped, her spirit undeterred. "Let's go, Vihaan"

As they moved through the crowd, Arhan's gaze lingered on Ammu, her laughter ringing out like the sweetest melody. He felt a strange tug at his heart, a feeling he couldn't quite place. Was it attraction? Curiosity? Or something deeper?

Vihaan steeled himself, trying to keep his composure. "Ammu, do you think you'll be happy?" he asked, his voice barely above a whisper.

"Of course! I want to build a life with Arhan," she said, her sincerity shining through. "I know he's a bit serious, but I believe we can find a way to laugh together."

Arhan's brow furrowed slightly. Did she really think they could laugh together? He felt a mix of emotions swirling inside him—fear, uncertainty, and an unexpected longing for connection.

"Let's take a picture!" Ammu exclaimed suddenly, pulling Vihaan and Arhan into a group. "Come on, smile!"

"Smile?" Arhan echoed, a hint of sarcasm in his voice. "You know I'm not a model, right?"

"Just try!" Ammu insisted, her enthusiasm infectious. With her bright eyes and wide grin, it was impossible not to feel a flicker of joy radiating from her.

As the camera flashed, Kethan snapped a candid shot of Arhan's reluctant smile, capturing the moment. "See? You can do it!" he teased, winking at his brother.

Arhan rolled his eyes but couldn't help the small grin that tugged at his lips. Maybe this wasn't so bad after all.

Vihaan watched from a distance, his heart heavy with regret. He had missed his chance with Ammu, and the realization stung. "Maybe next time," he whispered to himself, turning away from the scene.

Meanwhile, Nishan continued his playful banter with Ananya, the two of them lost in their own world. "You know," he said, leaning closer, "I think we'd make a great team. You, me, and a little adventure."

"Keep dreaming, Nishan," Ananya shot back, laughter dancing in her eyes. "You're more of a distraction than a partner."

As the evening wore on, the music swelled, laughter echoed, and the atmosphere buzzed with joy. Arhan found himself caught in a whirlwind of emotions, unsure of what the future held. But as he watched Ammu sparkle with life, he couldn't shake the feeling that perhaps, just perhaps, he was on the cusp of something beautiful.

"Here's to new beginnings," he murmured under his breath, watching Ammu light up the room, her laughter ringing like a promise of what was yet to come.

Chapter 6

Our Friendship

The grand hall was aglow with soft lights, the air thick with anticipation and the fragrance of fresh flowers. Laughter and chatter mingled as guests gathered to celebrate Ammu and Arhan's engagement. Amidst the swirling excitement, Ananya stood at the edge of the crowd, her heart racing. She had a plan to make this day unforgettable for her best friend.

Ammu was a whirlwind of energy, her eyes sparkling as she flitted from guest to guest, her laughter ringing like a bell. "Can you believe it, Ananya? I'm really getting engaged!" She twirled in her vibrant dress, the fabric swirling around her like a colorful cloud.

Ananya smiled, her heart swelling with affection for her friend. "I can! And you deserve every bit of happiness, Ammu."

As the evening wore on, the guests settled into their seats, and the emcee took the stage, announcing a special moment. "Ladies and gentlemen, we have a surprise speech from Ammu's best friend, Ananya!"

Ammu's eyes widened in disbelief. "What? No, Ananya! You don't have to!" But Ananya was already striding toward the microphone, her heart pounding with excitement and a hint of nerves.

"Hey, everyone!" she called, her voice steady as she scanned the crowd. "I just want to take a moment to talk about someone very special to me—my best friend, Ammu." She glanced at Ammu, whose cheeks flushed pink. "From the moment we met as kids, I knew we'd be inseparable. She's been my partner in crime, my confidante, and my sister. Every silly adventure we've had, every late-night chat, has made my life so much brighter."

Ammu's eyes glimmered with unshed tears, a mix of joy and embarrassment. "Stop it, Ananya! You're making me blush!"

Ananya continued, undeterred. "Ammu, you have this incredible ability to find joy in the simplest things. You've taught me to laugh at myself and to see the beauty in clumsiness. Remember that time we tried to bake a cake and ended up with a kitchen disaster? We laughed for hours!"

The crowd chuckled, picturing the scene, and Ammu covered her face with her hands, shaking her head in mock shame.

"Every moment with you has been a treasure," Ananya declared, her voice warm and sincere. "And I can't wait to see the joy you bring to Arhan's life. Together, you both will create beautiful memories."

A thunderous applause erupted, and Ammu's heart swelled. "Thank you, Ananya!" she called, her voice thick with emotion.

Just then, Vihaan stepped forward, his expression earnest. "If I may add a few words," he began, his voice slightly shaky. "Ammu is not just a friend; she's a beacon of light. Her kindness and laughter have touched everyone around her. I've seen her care for others genuinely, and that's something truly rare."

Ammu beamed at him, her heart fluttering at his praise.

"Honestly, there are countless times I've been a mess, but she always knows how to lift me up," Vihaan continued, glancing at Ammu. "And I'm grateful for every moment—every laugh, every shared secret."

"Aw, Vihaan!" Ammu exclaimed, her eyes shining. "You're going to make me cry!"

"Don't worry," Vihaan grinned, "the tears will just add to the cake we're going to eat later!"

The crowd laughed, and Vihaan gestured to the cake table. "Speaking of which, let's make this more fun. How about we pull Ammu into a song? Anyone up for it?"

Ammu's eyes widened again, and she clapped her hands. "Yes! I love dancing!"

The crowd cheered, and soon, a lively tune filled the air. Ananya and Vihaan pulled Ammu into the center, encouraging her to dance. "Come on, let's show them how it's done!"

As the music played, Ammu twirled and spun, her laughter infectious. Kethan, Priya, and Nishan joined in, moving to the rhythm and drawing others to the dance floor.

Arhan stood off to the side, his arms crossed, observing the joyous chaos. He felt a strange mix of admiration and confusion. Was it really possible that someone like Ammu could bring happiness to his life? Just then, Ananya spotted him and called out, "Arhan! Come join us!"

He shook his head, a polite smile on his face. "No, thank you. I'm not much of a dancer."

"Oh come on, it's just a little fun!" Ananya insisted, her eyes sparkling with mischief.

Ammu's gaze flickered to Arhan, a hint of disappointment in her eyes. "Please, Arhan? It would mean so much to me!"

Arhan hesitated, the pleading look in Ammu's eyes tugging at him. "I—"

"Just one dance! For Ammu!" Vihaan added, his voice light-hearted, trying to coax Arhan into joining.

"Alright, if it means that much to you," Arhan relented, stepping forward.

Ammu's face lit up with joy, and she clapped her hands. "Yes! Finally!"

As he joined the group, Kethan winked at Arhan. "See? Not so bad, right?"

The music swelled, and Ammu took Arhan's hand, pulling him into the dance. Their movements were awkward at first, but soon, they found a rhythm. Ammu laughed, her joy radiating off her, while Arhan tried to keep up, a bemused smile creeping onto his face.

"Not too bad," he admitted, his eyes sparkling with a newfound warmth as he looked at her.

"Just wait until we get to the cake!" Ammu teased, her laughter infectious.

After what felt like an eternity of dancing, the song ended, and everyone cheered. Arhan pulled Ammu close, their faces mere inches apart. "You really know how to throw a party, don't you?" he said, his tone teasing.

"I do my best!" she replied, her eyes sparkling with delight.

Just then, the dessert table came into view, a beautiful three-tiered cake standing tall, adorned with delicate flowers and elegant decorations. Ammu's eyes widened like a child's at a candy store. "Cake! I can't wait to share it with you!"

As they approached the table, Ammu picked up a fork, her excitement bubbling over. "Okay, I'm going to feed you first!"

"Wait, Ammu—" Arhan started, but she was already scooping up a generous piece of cake.

"Open wide!" she giggled, moving closer.

But just as she leaned in, she stumbled slightly, and the cake slipped from her grasp, splattering onto Arhan's shirt. "Oh no!" she gasped, her eyes going wide with horror.

"Seriously?" Arhan's voice was a mix of surprise and annoyance, though he struggled to keep his expression neutral as laughter erupted around them.

"I'm so sorry!" Ammu cried, her cheeks turning crimson. "I didn't mean to—"

"Looks like you've made quite the impression," Kethan joked, unable to contain his laughter.

Ammu covered her face with her hands, her mortification palpable. "This is so embarrassing!"

Arhan glanced down at his shirt, a slight frown creasing his brow. "Well, it's just cake," he said, trying to sound nonchalant, though he could feel the eyes of the guests on him.

"I'll clean it up! I promise!" Ammu exclaimed, her voice rising in panic.

"Relax, it's fine," Arhan replied, forcing a smile. He couldn't let his irritation show—not when everyone was watching. "It's just a little cake."

"Just a little?" Ammu echoed, biting her lip as she surveyed the mess. "I'll make it up to you, I swear!"

"You don't have to," he said, his tone softening slightly. "Let's just... enjoy the evening."

With a sheepish grin, Ammu nodded. "Okay. But I owe you one... or maybe two!"

As the party continued, laughter filled the air, and Arhan found himself laughing along with everyone else. Maybe this engagement wouldn't be so bad after all.

Kethan leaned over to him, a teasing glint in his eyes. "You know, it's moments like these that make life interesting. Just think of all the stories you'll get to tell!"

Arhan chuckled, shaking his head. "I suppose you're right. But I still expect you to help me get this cake off my shirt later."

"Deal!" Kethan replied, slapping him on the back.

As the evening flowed, the music played on, and the atmosphere buzzed with joy. Ammu, with her infectious laughter and unyielding spirit, had a way of making everything brighter. Arhan watched her dance, her carefree nature drawing him in. Maybe he could learn to bend just a little, especially around her.

As the night drew to a close, Arhan felt a warmth spreading through him, a feeling he had never expected to find in this arrangement. Perhaps there was more to this engagement than mere obligation. Perhaps there was a chance for something beautiful to blossom.

"Here's to new beginnings," he whispered to himself, smiling as he watched Ammu dance, her laughter ringing like a promise of love yet to come.

Chapter 7

The Realization

The grand hall was now quieting down, the remnants of laughter and chatter fading into whispers as the guests began to disperse. Arhan leaned against a marble pillar, his arms crossed, surveying the aftermath of the celebration. The vibrant decorations were still twinkling, but his mood was anything but festive.

"Can you believe that?" Kethan chuckled, joining him. "Your fiancée just launched a piece of cake at you. What a way to start a marriage!"

Arhan rolled his eyes, irritation creeping into his voice. "It's embarrassing. She's... clumsy. I can't be seen like this."

"Clumsy? That's an understatement. She's like a walking disaster zone," Kethan laughed, shaking his head. "But honestly, you could use a little chaos in your life. You're far too serious."

Arhan frowned, his gaze drifting over to where Ammu was giggling with Ananya, her laughter ringing out like a melody. "I'm serious because I have to be. I don't need someone who's going to trip over her own feet every time she walks into a room."

Kethan raised an eyebrow, his teasing tone turning slightly serious. "Come on, man. You can't deny she has a certain... charm. She's got this brightness that lights up the room. You might want to give her a chance."

"I don't have time for this," Arhan replied, his voice flat, but he couldn't shake the image of Ammu, her carefree spirit contrasting sharply with his rigid demeanor. "This is just an arrangement. I'm not looking for a partner who'll create more problems."

"Problems? Like cake on your shirt?" Kethan smirked. "Please, you need to lighten up. You might actually enjoy life a little more."

"Maybe if this whole thing didn't feel like a trap," Arhan muttered, running a hand through his hair. "I didn't ask for this marriage. It's just... not me."

Ammu, standing a few feet away, froze as she caught snippets of their conversation. Clumsy? Not his type? She felt a knot tighten in her stomach. She wasn't one to back down from a fight, especially when it involved her dignity.

"Excuse me?" Her voice sliced through the air, drawing both men's attention.

Arhan blinked, momentarily taken aback by the fiery determination in Ammu's eyes. "Ammu, I—"

"Don't you dare say another word!" she interrupted, her tone sharp. "You think I'm clumsy and a nuisance? Well, guess what? I don't need your approval or your pity!"

Kethan stifled a laugh, clearly entertained by the unexpected turn of events. Arhan's expression shifted from surprise to annoyance, his brows knitting together.

"You're being dramatic," he replied, his voice cool.

"Dramatic?" Ammu's voice rose, her hands on her hips. "I'm just standing here, defending myself against your ridiculous assumptions! You think you're so much better than me just because you have a fancy title and a posh office?"

"I never said that," Arhan shot back, his patience waning. "But marriage is about partnership, and I don't see how you expect to fit in mine if you can't even keep your balance."

"Maybe I don't want to fit in!" Ammu retorted, her cheeks flushed with anger. "Maybe I'd rather trip and fall than pretend to be someone I'm not. You think you can just stand there and judge me? Well, newsflash, Arhan: I'm not perfect, and I don't want to be!"

"Then what do you want?" His tone softened, but the challenge still lingered in his eyes.

"I want to be respected!" she declared, her voice unwavering. "I want to be seen for who I am, not just your clumsy little wife who doesn't deserve you."

"Maybe you're right," he replied, stepping closer, his voice low and serious. "Maybe we both deserve better."

Their eyes locked, and for a moment, the world around them faded, leaving just the two of them amidst the chaos of the party. But then, Ammu's frustration bubbled over, and she turned sharply, her dress catching on the edge of a nearby table.

"Whoa!" she yelped, her arms flailing as she lost her balance.

In an instant, Arhan lunged forward, his reflexes kicking in. He caught her waist just before she fell, but as he steadied her, she pushed away. "I don't need your help!" she exclaimed defiantly.

"Are you sure about that?" he asked, a hint of disbelief creeping into his voice.

"Absolutely!" Ammu shot back, her pride refusing to let her show any vulnerability. But just as she took a step back, her foot slipped on a stray napkin, and down she went, landing with a soft thud on the floor.

A collective gasp echoed through the hall as a few guests turned to watch. "Ammu!" Arhan exclaimed, rushing to her side, concern etched across his face.

"I'm fine!" she huffed, pushing herself up, her cheeks burning with embarrassment. "This is ridiculous. I can't believe I'm even fighting with you!"

"Then stop it!" Arhan snapped, his voice rising. "You're making a scene!"

"Maybe I want to make a scene!" she shouted back, her temper flaring. "You think you can just dismiss me? I won't be another trophy on your shelf, Arhan!"

"Then what do you expect from me? To coddle you like a child?" he challenged, his frustration bubbling over.

"Maybe I want you to treat me like an equal!" she shot back, her eyes flashing with determination.

Their argument echoed through the hall, drawing the attention of curious guests. Ammu's heart raced as she realized how far they had spiraled into this petty feud. Just then, she caught sight of her parents, standing by the dessert table, their faces lit with pride and joy at the celebration.

Suddenly, her anger faltered, replaced by a wave of guilt. How could she call off their marriage when her parents were so happy? She glanced at Arhan, who looked equally conflicted, his expression softening as he caught her gaze.

"Maybe we both need to cool off," he suggested, his tone less confrontational. "This isn't how I envisioned our engagement."

Ammu nodded, her heart pounding. "Right. I'll just... pretend I didn't hear what you said. For my parents' sake."

"Same here," he muttered, crossing his arms, his frustration giving way to something else—an understanding, perhaps.

As they stood in silence, the atmosphere around them shifted. The laughter and chatter resumed, a distant hum that felt oddly comforting despite the tension between them. Ammu took a deep breath, forcing a smile as she turned to her parents.

"Everything okay, sweetie?" her mother asked, concern etching her features.

"Just a little disagreement," Ammu replied, her voice light, masking the turmoil inside. "Nothing to worry about!"

Her father chuckled, oblivious to the undercurrents. "That's normal for newlyweds, right?"

"Right," Arhan echoed, his voice flat, but his eyes glinted with something that resembled amusement.

Ammu shot him a look, but he merely shrugged, a hint of a smile threatening to break through. She couldn't help but feel the corners of her own lips twitching.

"Let's just enjoy the evening, shall we?" Kethan chimed in, eager to diffuse the tension. "Cake, dance, and lots of laughter! Who's in?"

"I'm in!" Ammu declared, her spirit lifting as she joined her friends, feigning a sense of normalcy.

The group began to disperse, laughter ringing through the hall once more, but the chip on Ammu's shoulder remained. She had entered into this engagement with dreams and hopes, but now, with the harsh reality of Arhan's words echoing in her mind, those dreams felt tainted.

As the night wore on, she found herself glancing at Arhan from time to time, their earlier spat hanging between them like a fragile thread. He was handsome, but the arrogance that initially drew her to him now felt suffocating, a weight upon her shoulders.

"Hey!" Ananya called, pulling Ammu back to reality. "Let's dance! You can't let a little cake mess ruin the fun!"

"Right!" Ammu smiled, forcing herself to join in the merriment, but her heart wasn't fully in it. The laughter felt distant, almost echoing through a tunnel.

Arhan watched her, a sense of unease settling in his chest. Ammu had brought a light into his life he never knew he needed, but now, that light felt dimmed by the weight of expectations and misunderstandings. As he joined the others on the dance floor, he caught her eye, and for a brief moment, the tension faded.

"Let's just get through this," he thought, forcing a smile as he twirled with his friends, but the nagging feeling remained. What had started as an obligation was now a battleground of emotions.

Maybe he could learn to appreciate her clumsiness, he mused, but for now, it seemed like a long road ahead.

As the music swelled, Ammu danced, her laughter mingling with the crowd, but with each spin, she felt the distance between them grow. Perhaps their marriage was just a stage, and they were merely playing roles—two actors in a comedy of errors, waiting for the curtain to fall

Chapter 8

Maybe

The morning sun poured through the window, casting warm rays across Ammu's room. She sat on the edge of her bed, her heart heavy with uncertainty. The events of last night replayed in her mind like a loop, and despite the laughter and fun, the argument with Arhan hovered over her, dark and brooding.

Her phone buzzed, jolting her from her thoughts. A message from Arhan popped up: "Meet me at Café Delights at noon. We need to talk."

Ammu sighed, twisting a strand of hair around her finger. The thought of facing him again sent a shiver down her spine. "What more could he possibly want?" she muttered to herself. But after a moment's hesitation, she typed back a quick response: "Okay. I'll be there."

As she stepped into the bustling café, the aroma of freshly brewed coffee enveloped her like a comforting blanket. She spotted Arhan sitting at a corner table, his posture rigid, eyes scanning the menu as if it held the secrets of the universe. The contrast between his sharp suit and the cozy, relaxed vibe of the café made her stomach churn.

"Hi," she said, forcing a smile as she slid into the seat across from him.

He looked up, his expression unreadable. "Thanks for coming."

"I didn't have much of a choice," she replied, crossing her arms defensively. "What do you want to discuss?"

Arhan set the menu down, his gaze steady. "I think we need to talk about... us. Our marriage."

Ammu raised an eyebrow, her heart pounding. "Us? More like a corporate merger," she quipped, trying to lighten the mood, but it fell flat. "You're a machine, Arhan. All you do is work. What do you even know about love?"

His jaw tightened, but he didn't flinch. "I know enough to understand that we need to find a way to make this work. My parents expect us to be happy together."

"Happy? You mean pretending, right? Because I can't see myself living with someone who treats life like a spreadsheet," she shot back, her frustration bubbling over. "I refuse to be part of a loveless arrangement."

"Then what do you suggest?" he asked, his tone calm but edged with irritation. "You want a solution? I have one."

Ammu leaned forward, intrigued despite herself. "What do you mean?"

He pulled out a neatly folded document from his briefcase, placing it on the table between them. "A marriage agreement. I've outlined the do's and don'ts for our relationship."

Ammu blinked at the paper, then back at him. "You're kidding, right?" she said, incredulity painting her features. "You can't be serious!"

"I am serious," Arhan replied, his voice steady. "If we are going to go through with this, we need to establish some ground rules. It'll help us avoid unnecessary conflicts."

She picked up the agreement, scanning the bullet points. "No emotional attachment, maintain separate lives, and agree to meet weekly to review our progress?" Ammu shook her head in disbelief. "Is this really how you want to start a marriage?"

"Consider it a temporary measure," he said, leaning back in his chair, his expression unwavering. "We can pretend to be happy until the wedding, then live as strangers in the same house. It's practical."

"Practical? This isn't a business deal, Arhan! This is my life!" Ammu exclaimed, her voice rising. "You can't just reduce love to a checklist."

"Maybe I can," he countered, his eyes narrowing slightly. "Look, if we don't do this, we'll end up resenting each other. This way, we maintain our independence while keeping up appearances."

Ammu sighed, frustration and sadness swirling inside her. She wanted to argue more, but a part of her recognized the logic behind his proposal. "So, you want me to play house with you while we act like everything is perfect?"

"Exactly," he replied, his voice firm. "It's a compromise, Ammu. We can make this work."

She chewed on her lip, the weight of his words sinking in. "And what if I can't do it? What if I can't pretend to be happy?"

"Then we'll revisit this agreement," he said, his tone softer now. "But I think you can. You're strong-willed, and I respect that. Just give it time."

Ammu stared at him, searching for any sign of sincerity. "You really think this will work?"

"Honestly?" He hesitated, then nodded. "I think it's worth a shot. We can create a comfortable arrangement, at least until we figure each other out."

"Fine," she said, her voice barely above a whisper. "I'll try it your way. But if I start feeling like a trophy wife, I'm out."

"Deal." He extended a hand across the table, and after a moment of hesitation, she took it, a strange mix of resolve and apprehension coursing through her.

The café buzzed around them, but in that moment, it felt like they were the only two people in the world. As they wrapped up their meeting, Ammu's heart felt heavy, but she knew there was no turning back now.

When she returned home, her mind was racing. She tossed her bag on the bed and collapsed beside it, tears pooling in her eyes as the reality of the situation hit her. This wasn't the fairytale she had dreamt of, filled with romance and laughter. No, this was a carefully orchestrated performance, and she was the lead actress in a play that felt all too real.

"Why did I think it would be different?" she whispered to herself, her heart aching. "Why did I let myself believe this would be anything but a business arrangement?"

Just then, the door creaked open, and Priya stepped in, her brows furrowing in concern when she saw Ammu's tear-streaked face. "Ammu, what happened? Why are you crying?"

Ammu quickly wiped her eyes, forcing a smile that felt more like a grimace. "Oh, it's nothing. I'm just... going to miss everyone," she lied, her voice trembling.

Priya's expression shifted from concern to confusion. "Miss everyone? But you just got married! You're supposed to be happy!"

"I know," Ammu sighed, her heart heavy with the burden of her deception. "It's just… everything is changing so fast. I thought I'd have a fairy tale, and now…"

"Now what?" Priya pressed gently, her eyes searching Ammu's.

"Now it feels like I'm walking into a trap," Ammu admitted, her voice cracking. "I don't want to be just a name on a document, Priya. I want to be loved, not just tolerated."

Priya knelt beside her, wrapping an arm around Ammu's shoulders. "You deserve love, Ammu. But you also need to give it time. Maybe he'll surprise you."

"Surprise me?" Ammu scoffed, wiping her tears away. "He's a corporate machine! He doesn't know the first thing about love."

"Give him a chance," Priya urged, her tone soothing. "People can change. You just need to find the right way to connect with him."

"I don't know if I can," Ammu whispered, her heart aching with the weight of her expectations. "What if I end up losing myself in this?"

"You won't," Priya said firmly. "Just be yourself, and don't lose sight of what you want. You have to fight for your happiness, Ammu. Don't let anyone dictate what your love story should be."

Ammu nodded slowly, absorbing her sister's comforting words. "You're right. I just need to stay true to myself, no matter what."

"Exactly! Now, how about we plan a little surprise for Arhan? Something to shake up the corporate machine a bit?" Priya suggested, a playful grin breaking through the seriousness of the moment.

Ammu chuckled, warmth flooding her heart. "Okay, I'm listening. What do you have in mind?"

As Priya began to outline an outrageous plan involving spontaneous adventures and silly challenges for Arhan, Ammu couldn't help but feel a flicker of hope. Maybe, just maybe, she could find a way to make this work, even if it meant navigating through the chaos of their unconventional arrangement.

And as laughter filled the room, the tears began to dry, leaving behind a sense of determination—a promise to herself that she wouldn't give up on her dreams of love, no matter how tangled the path ahead might be

Chapter 9

The Wedding Day

The sun hung high in the sky, casting a golden glow over the grand venue adorned with flowers and colorful drapes. The air buzzed with excitement as guests filled the hall, laughter and chatter blending in a sweet symphony. Ammu stood in front of the mirror, adorned in a stunning red lehenga that contrasted beautifully with her dusky skin. Her heart raced, a mix of anticipation and dread swirling within her. This was the day she had envisioned since childhood—a day filled with love and joy. But today felt different; it felt like stepping into a carefully choreographed dance she hadn't chosen.

"Ammu! You look like a princess!" Ananya squealed, bouncing into the room with her phone raised to capture the moment. Ammu turned, forcing a smile even as her stomach twisted. "More like a pawn in a game," she murmured under her breath.

"Stop that! Today is your day. No negativity allowed!" Ananya playfully nudged her shoulder. "You'll be fine. Just think about how happy your dad is."

Ammu glanced toward the window, where she could see her father, Hemanth, chatting animatedly with guests, a proud smile plastered on his face. "He looks so happy," she whispered, and a small smile broke through her uncertainty.

"See? You can do this. Just think of him," Ananya encouraged, giving her a reassuring pat before stepping back to admire her friend. "Make him proud, Ammu. It's not just about you; it's about family."

As the minutes ticked by, Ammu felt a knot form in her chest. She glanced at her phone, a message from Arhan lingering in her mind. "See you at the altar." It felt so clinical—like a business meeting rather than the union of two souls. She had agreed to this arrangement, but the weight of it pressed heavily on her.

Before she could spiral into her thoughts, Kethan, Arhan's brother and personal secretary, entered the room. "Hey, Ammu, you look stunning," he said, his voice warm but tinged with a hint of seriousness. "Just... be patient with Arhan. He's not as tough as he seems."

Ammu raised an eyebrow, skepticism evident. "Really? Because he's acting like I'm a spreadsheet and he's just checking off boxes."

Kethan chuckled lightly, shaking his head. "He can be a bit rigid, but he's got a good heart. Just remember, being clumsy isn't a crime. He might surprise you."

"Surprise me?" Ammu echoed, her voice laced with doubt. "He's not exactly known for spontaneous gestures."

"True, but he's trying," Kethan asserted, his eyes serious now. "Give him a chance. Today is important for both of you."

With a reluctant nod, Ammu turned back to the mirror, her heart racing as the moment approached.

The music shifted, signaling that the ceremony was about to begin. Ananya helped adjust Ammu's dupatta, her hands trembling slightly with excitement. "You ready?" she asked, her eyes sparkling with anticipation.

"Ready or not, here I come," Ammu replied, trying to sound confident but failing to mask the tremor in her voice.

As she stepped out to join the procession, the sight of Arhan waiting at the altar took her breath away. Dressed in an elegant sherwani, he looked every bit the part of a CEO—a powerful figure. But today, he seemed distant, his expression guarded as he waited for her.

"Wow," Nishan muttered, standing by Arhan's side. "You clean up nice, boss."

Arhan shot him a sidelong glance, but his eyes were drawn back to Ammu. For a fleeting moment, something flickered in his gaze—an appreciation, perhaps? Ammu's heart fluttered, but the weight of their agreement loomed large.

As she approached, Arhan's posture shifted slightly, a hint of softness breaking through his stern facade. She met his eyes, trying to convey her uncertainty. This wasn't how she had imagined it, yet here they were, two strangers bound by a contract.

"Let's get this over with," he murmured under his breath, barely loud enough for her to hear.

The priest began the ceremony, chanting mantras that echoed through the hall. Ammu felt her father's proud gaze on her as he stood beside her, his hand resting gently on her shoulder. "You're doing great, sweetheart," he whispered, squeezing her hand.

"Thanks, Dad," she replied, hoping to quell the turmoil within her.

As the priest instructed Arhan to tie the sacred knots around her neck, Ammu felt a mix of excitement and despair. This was the moment that would seal their agreement—an agreement that felt more like a cage than a blessing. She could feel Arhan's hands tremble slightly as he tied the first knot, his brows furrowing in concentration.

"You okay?" she asked softly, trying to break the tension.

"Just... focused," Arhan replied, his voice barely above a whisper.

A muffled laugh escaped from Nishan, who leaned in closer. "At least you don't have to worry about tripping over your own feet today, Ammu," he teased, trying to lighten the mood.

Ammu shot him a glare, her heart racing. "Don't jinx it!" she hissed, earning a chuckle from both men.

The priest continued, his voice rising over the gathered crowd, "With this knot, you are bound together for eternity!"

Ammu's heart sank as the realization hit her. Eternity? In a marriage built on terms and conditions?

As the final knot was tied, her father stepped forward, his eyes shimmering with emotion. "Arhan, please take care of my little girl. I've pampered her a lot, and I hope you will do the same," he said, his voice thick with sentiment.

"Of course, sir," Arhan replied, his tone sincere. "I'll make sure she's taken care of."

Ammu felt a strange mix of relief and frustration at his words. Did he mean it? Or was it just part of the act?

As the ceremony concluded, the crowd erupted into cheers, and Ammu felt herself being swept up in the moment. She posed for photographs, her cheeks sore from smiling, but inside, her heart was heavy.

"Look at you! The beautiful bride!" Ananya squealed, practically bouncing beside her as they posed for yet another picture.

"Yeah, beautiful but confused," Ammu muttered under her breath, trying to maintain her composure.

"Hey, it's a new beginning!" Ananya chirped as she pulled Ammu in for a hug. "Just embrace it!"

As they made their way to the reception, Ammu's heart felt like a pendulum, swinging between hope and despair. The venue was beautifully decorated, a kaleidoscope of colors and sounds. As the couple entered, the guests erupted in applause, and Ammu forced herself to wave, even as she felt like a marionette on a string.

"I can't believe you actually went through with it!" Nishan teased as he approached, a playful smirk on his face. "How does it feel to be Mrs. Corporate Machine?"

"I feel like I'm in a sitcom," Ammu deadpanned, rolling her eyes. "Where's my laugh track?"

Nishan laughed heartily, leaning closer. "Honestly, though, Arhan's not as bad as he seems. Just give him some time. I think he might actually care."

"Care?" Ammu scoffed, glancing at Arhan, who was engrossed in conversation with their parents. "I think he cares more about profits than people."

"Don't underestimate him," Nishan insisted, his voice dropping to a conspiratorial whisper. "I know about the agreement. But he's trying, Ammu. Just... let him find his way."

With a sigh, Ammu took a sip from her drink, the fizzy carbonation sending a shiver down her spine. "I just don't want to be a footnote in his life story," she confessed, her voice barely above a whisper.

"You won't be," Nishan reassured her. "Just keep being the clumsy, vibrant girl you are. Maybe that will shake him out of his corporate shell."

The evening wore on, and Ammu felt herself slipping into the rhythm of the celebration. The laughter, the music, the twinkling lights—it was enchanting, even as her heart struggled to reconcile her reality.

As the night deepened, she caught Arhan watching her from across the room. There was something in his gaze— an intensity that made her stomach flutter, but she quickly reminded herself of the agreement that loomed over them.

"Want me to get you a drink?" Ananya asked, nudging her gently.

"Sure," Ammu replied, her gaze still locked on Arhan.

"Just remember, he's not all bad," Ananya added, slipping away into the crowd.

Ammu took a deep breath, trying to gather her thoughts. She had entered this marriage with so many expectations, but now it all felt like a balancing act on a tightrope.

"Hey," Arhan's voice cut through her thoughts, and she turned to face him. "You're stunning tonight."

"Thanks," she replied, trying to gauge his expression. "You clean up nice too."

He chuckled softly, a sound that felt foreign yet warm. "I guess we both look the part."

She hesitated, searching for the right words. "How do you feel about all of this?"

"Honestly?" Arhan paused, his gaze steady. "I'm still figuring it out. But seeing you like this... it's made me rethink a lot."

Ammu's heart raced at his admission. "Rethink what?"

"Rethink the agreement," he admitted, his voice low. "Maybe there's more to this than just a contract."

Her breath caught in her throat. "You mean that?"

He nodded slowly, his gaze unwavering. "I do. I just need time to process everything."

"Time," she echoed, her heart swelling with hope. "I can do that."

As they stood there, surrounded by laughter and celebration, Ammu felt a flicker of something—something that might just grow into the love she had always dreamed of. Maybe today wasn't just a performance after all; maybe it was the beginning of something unexpected, a story that was uniquely theirs, with all its chaos and beauty.

And as they took their first steps into their new life together, Ammu couldn't shake the feeling that perhaps, just perhaps, they would find their way through the tangled mess of expectations and agreements. Because in the end, love was worth fighting for, even if it started with a clumsy agreement.

Chapter 10

Vihaan's Feelings

The sun dipped low in the Mumbai skyline, casting long shadows across the bustling streets. The vibrant sounds of the city echoed in the background, blending with the music wafting from the reception hall where laughter and chatter spilled out like a bubbling fountain. Inside, the grand venue buzzed with energy, adorned with twinkling lights and colorful floral arrangements.

Arhan leaned against a plush wall, his mind racing. He had just stepped away from the crowd, needing a moment to himself amidst the clamor. He watched as guests danced, their joy infectious, but his thoughts were tangled. He caught sight of Ammu across the room, her laughter ringing out like music, her eyes sparkling with joy. But then his gaze shifted to Vihaan and Priya, standing a little too close for comfort. His chest tightened.

"Are you really going to miss her that much?" Vihaan's voice floated toward Arhan, cutting through the chatter.

"Of course! I mean, who else is going to keep you grounded?" Priya chuckled lightly. Arhan felt a flicker of annoyance. The way Vihaan leaned in, his expression sincere, made Arhan's stomach twist.

"I just wish I had told her how much she means to me before it was too late," Vihaan confessed, his tone earnest, the wistfulness in his voice palpable. Arhan's jaw clenched as he listened, feeling an unfamiliar heat rise in his chest.

"Vihaan, it's not like she's gone anywhere," Priya replied, her voice soothing. "You're still close. Just tell her how you feel. She deserves to know."

"What if she doesn't feel the same?" Vihaan countered, a hint of desperation creeping in. "What if I've waited too long?"

Arhan's heart raced, jealousy flaring up like a fire ignited by a careless match. He didn't want to hear this. Ammu was his wife, even if it was just an agreement. The thought of someone else expressing feelings for her twisted something deep within him. "I should just go back," he muttered under his breath. But his feet stayed planted, as if glued to the floor.

"Hey, you," Ammu's voice broke through, light and cheerful. She appeared at his side, her smile brightening the dim corner. "What are you doing hiding over here?"

He straightened, forcing a casual demeanor. "Just taking a breather." He glanced back at Vihaan and Priya, who were now engaged in a hushed conversation, their expressions serious.

"What were they talking about?" Ammu asked, her brow furrowing slightly.

"Nothing important," Arhan replied, trying to dismiss it with a wave of his hand. "Just typical party chatter."

"Are you sure?" she pressed, her curiosity piqued. "It didn't look typical. You know Vihaan, right? He gets all serious sometimes."

Arhan hesitated, the image of Vihaan confessing his feelings still fresh in his mind. "He was just saying he's going to miss your sister. She's moving away for a while, right?"

Ammu's eyes narrowed slightly, clearly not satisfied with the answer. "Moving away? Priya didn't mention that to me."

"Maybe it's nothing," Arhan suggested, trying to steer the conversation away. "Let's focus on us, huh?"

Ammu's expression softened, but the concern lingered. "I just want to make sure everyone is okay. Vihaan has always been a good friend to me."

"Yeah, well, sometimes friends can get too... attached," he replied, feeling a twinge of annoyance.

"Are you jealous?" she teased, a playful glint in her eyes.

"Me? No," he scoffed, though the heat in his cheeks betrayed him. "I just think he should respect the boundaries."

"Boundaries?" Ammu echoed, crossing her arms, a smile dancing on her lips. "Or are you just worried about him getting to know me better?"

Arhan shifted on his feet, suddenly aware of how close they were standing. "It's not like that," he insisted, though the defensive edge in his voice only made her grin widen.

"Sure, Mr. CEO," she laughed, nudging him playfully. "You're not as tough as you pretend to be."

He couldn't help but chuckle, the tension from earlier dissipating. "I just... don't want you to get hurt."

"Aw, that's sweet," she said, her tone teasing yet sincere. "But I can take care of myself. Besides, I'm not a fragile thing."

"Yeah, I've seen you trip over your own feet more times than I can count," he shot back, smirking.

"Hey! That's not fair!" Ammu exclaimed, her laughter ringing out like a bell. "I'm just... gracefully challenged."

"Gracefully challenged, huh?" he mused, a smile creeping onto his face. "I'll give you that."

The atmosphere around them shifted, the intensity of their earlier conversation fading into something lighter.

But as Ammu's laughter faded, he noticed her gaze flicker back to Priya and Vihaan.

"Do you think they're okay?" she asked, her voice softening.

Arhan followed her gaze, his heart sinking slightly. "Yeah, they're fine. Just... talking."

"Talking," she repeated, her brow furrowing again. "It didn't look like just talking."

"Trust me, Ammu. Sometimes people just need to have a conversation. You don't need to worry about it," he replied, a hint of frustration seeping through.

She turned to look at him, her expression serious. "But you do worry about me, don't you?"

His breath caught for a moment. "Of course, I do. You're my wife, aren't you?"

"Just an agreement, remember?" she replied, her voice a mix of playfulness and sincerity. "What happens if we don't make it past this contract?"

Arhan's heart raced. "That's not going to happen," he declared, the fierceness of his words surprising even himself. "We will make it work."

"Really?" she asked, her eyes wide with hope. "You mean that?"

"I wouldn't say it if I didn't mean it," he replied firmly, taking a step closer. "I'm committed to making this work, Ammu. You're worth it."

She smiled softly, the tension easing between them. "Maybe we just need to find our rhythm, then."

"Rhythm," he echoed, the word rolling off his tongue. "Yeah, let's do that."

As they stood together, the noise of the celebration faded into the background, their connection deepening. And for a moment, the world outside melted away, leaving only the two of them and the unspoken promise of something more.

"Hey, dance with me," Ammu suddenly suggested, her eyes sparkling with mischief.

"Dance? Here?" Arhan raised an eyebrow, glancing around at the crowd.

"Why not?" she challenged, tugging at his hand. "Come on, it'll be fun!"

Arhan hesitated, but the infectious energy of her excitement pulled him in. "Alright, but only for a moment."

Ammu grinned widely and led him to the makeshift dance floor, the music thrumming beneath their feet. She twirled, her lehenga flying around her like petals in the wind. He couldn't help but laugh, the sound bubbling up from deep within him.

"See? This isn't so bad," she beamed, pulling him into the rhythm.

"Just don't step on my toes, alright?" he warned, trying to maintain some semblance of composure.

"Me? Never!" she exclaimed, a mock innocence in her tone. But as they began to sway together, it was clear that the playful challenge of their movements was a dance of its own.

With each step, the earlier tension melted away, leaving only the joy of their connection. And as Arhan watched Ammu lose herself in the moment, he realized that maybe, just maybe, this arrangement was turning into something he hadn't expected. Something worth fighting for.

As the music swelled, drowning out the world around them, Arhan held her close, feeling the warmth radiating from her. "I think I'm starting to understand this whole partnership thing," he murmured, his voice barely above the melody.

"Good," Ammu replied, her smile radiant. "Because I'm not going anywhere."

And in that moment, surrounded by laughter and love, Arhan knew he was ready to embrace whatever came next, even if it meant facing the chaos of their lives together.

Chapter 11

Their First Night

The morning sun spilled into the newlywed home, illuminating the modest yet charming space that Arhan had gifted Ammu as a wedding present. Cream-colored walls were adorned with framed photos of their wedding day, capturing the laughter and joy of that whirlwind celebration. Arhan stood by the window, hands shoved deep into his pockets, watching the bustling streets of Mumbai come to life. He felt an odd mix of satisfaction and apprehension.

"Wow, if this isn't a fairy tale, I don't know what is!" Ammu's voice broke through his thoughts, her cheerful presence contrasting sharply with the seriousness that often clouded his mind.

He turned to find her leaning against the kitchen counter, an oversized t-shirt draping over her petite frame, her hair a tousled halo around her face, still slightly sleepy but radiant. She was holding a glass of milk, and despite the ordinary beverage, the sight made his heart skip. "It's just a house, Ammu. We'll make it a home together," he replied, trying to keep his tone light.

She laughed, the sound echoing warmly off the walls. "Just a house? Look at it! It has potential!" She took a sip of her milk, her eyes sparkling. "And I promise to add my charm to it. Just wait and see!"

"Charm, huh? You mean organized chaos?" he teased, smirking as he remembered her clumsiness from the wedding. She had tripped over her lehenga during their first dance, leaving him both amused and slightly panicked.

"Hey! I prefer to think of it as spontaneous creativity!" Ammu shot back, mock indignation lining her features. "Besides, I'm sure you need more fun in your life, Mr. CEO."

Arhan chuckled, shaking his head. "I think I'll manage without your 'spontaneous creativity.'"

"Suit yourself! But you're going to miss out on so much fun!" Ammu pouted playfully.

"Okay, okay! I'll try to embrace the chaos," he conceded, his tone lightening.

Just then, the doorbell rang, interrupting their banter. "I'll get it!" Ammu exclaimed, bounding toward the door, her excitement palpable. She opened it to reveal Priya, her twin sister, standing there with misty eyes and a bouquet of flowers.

"Priya! What are you doing here?" Ammu's delight quickly turned to concern as she noticed her sister's tear-streaked cheeks.

"I just... I can't believe you're actually married," Priya admitted, her voice trembling. "It feels so surreal. I'm going to miss you so much."

Ammu rushed forward, enveloping her sister in a tight embrace. "Oh, Priya! I'm going to miss you too! But we'll still be close. You can come over anytime!"

"I know, but it's not the same!" Priya pulled back, wiping away her tears with a sniffle. "You've always been my partner in crime. It's hard to think of you starting a new life without me."

Arhan stood awkwardly by the window, unsure if he should intervene or let the sisters have their moment. He felt a pang of guilt at the thought of taking Ammu away from her sister.

Before he could decide, Kethan, Arhan's brother and personal secretary, walked in. "Hey, ladies! What's with the tears? This is supposed to be a joyous occasion!" He flashed a charming smile, trying to lighten the mood.

"Can you not see? Ammu is leaving me!" Priya wailed, throwing her hands up in melodramatic fashion.

Kethan approached Priya, gently placing a hand on her shoulder. "You know, Ammu will always be your sister.

Just because she's married doesn't mean she's gone. And besides," he continued, his voice softening, "I promise to look after her. For your sake."

Priya's expression shifted, a small smile teasing at her lips. "You really mean that?"

"Absolutely. I'll keep her safe and sound. I have a reputation to protect," he winked, and Priya couldn't help but laugh, her sadness momentarily forgotten.

"Okay, okay! I'll stop crying," she replied, her mood lifting. "But I'm still going to call you every day!"

"Deal," Ammu agreed, pulling her sister in for another hug.

As they parted, Priya glanced at Arhan, her gaze flickering with uncertainty. "And you... you better take care of my sister. No funny business, alright?"

Arhan raised an eyebrow, a smirk playing on his lips. "No funny business? I'll try my best, but it's not like I can control her clumsiness."

Ammu elbowed him playfully. "Hey! I can be graceful when I want to be!"

"Sure you can," Arhan teased back, the warmth in his eyes a stark contrast to his usual stoic demeanor.

The sisters shared a laugh, and for a moment, the air was light and joyful. But as the moment faded, Priya's expression turned serious again. "Just promise me you'll keep in touch, Ammu. I don't want to feel like I've lost you."

"I promise," Ammu said, her voice steady. "You'll always be my sister, no matter where I am."

With Priya finally feeling reassured, the goodbyes were bittersweet. Kethan offered to help Priya with her things, ushering her out while Ammu watched with a heavy heart.

"Don't be sad, Ammu. This is a new beginning for both of us," Kethan said softly, giving her a reassuring smile.

"I know... it just feels different," she admitted, a hint of nostalgia creeping into her voice.

As the door clicked shut behind them, Arhan turned to Ammu, who was now staring out the window, her thoughts distant. "You okay?" he asked, concern lacing his tone.

"Yeah, just... taking it all in," she replied, turning to him with a soft smile. "It's a big change."

"Change can be good," he said, stepping closer. "And we'll figure this out together."

"Right! Together!" Ammu agreed, her eyes lighting up again.

That evening, as the sun dipped below the horizon, casting a warm golden glow through their new home, the atmosphere was charged with anticipation. With their families gathered for the first-night ceremony, the house buzzed with energy.

Arhan watched from the sidelines as Ammu was fussed over by her mother and aunts, delighting in the traditional rituals. He felt a warm flutter in his chest as he observed her vibrant spirit light up the room.

"Are you ready?" Nishan teased, nudging Arhan as they stood off to the side. "Looks like you've got competition in the charm department."

"Very funny," Arhan muttered, his eyes never leaving Ammu. "I'm just... waiting."

"Waiting for what? The grand reveal?" Nishan's grin widened. "Come on, man. It's just a ceremony."

"Yeah, well, it's more than just a ceremony for her," Arhan replied, his voice low. "She deserves to feel special."

Nishan raised an eyebrow. "You're not thinking of romance, are you? It's just an agreement, remember?"

"Tell that to my heart," Arhan grumbled, irritated at how much Ammu was getting under his skin.

Finally, the moment arrived, and the ceremony unfolded in a beautiful display of tradition. Ammu donned a stunning outfit, a shimmering new lehenga that accentuated her beauty. Arhan's breath hitched as she entered the room.

"Wow," he breathed, unable to tear his gaze away.

Ammu caught his eye, and her cheeks flushed pink. "Is it too much?"

"Not at all," he replied, his voice barely above a whisper. "You look... incredible."

"Thanks!" she grinned, her excitement bubbling over. "Now, where's my husband?"

Arhan chuckled, shaking his head. "Right here, waiting for you."

As the night wore on, the guests dispersed, leaving just the two of them in the quiet of their new home. Ammu took a deep breath, the laughter from earlier still lingering in the air. "So, what now?"

He glanced around, feeling the weight of their new reality settle in. "I guess we... see how this goes?"

"Right! So, how about some milk?" she suggested playfully, holding up the glass she'd brought earlier. "Milk before bed is a must!"

He laughed, the warmth of the moment wrapping around them like a cozy blanket. "Only if you promise not to spill it everywhere."

"Challenge accepted!" Ammu declared, winking before taking a sip.

As they settled in for the night, Ammu placed a couple of pillows between them on the bed, her expression mischievous. "Just to make sure we keep things comfortable, you know?"

Arhan raised an eyebrow, a smirk playing on his lips. "Comfortable, huh? You think I'm going to attack you in your sleep?"

"Hey! You never know!" she shot back, laughter spilling from her lips.

But as they prepared for bed, Arhan felt a swirl of emotions he couldn't quite name. He watched as Ammu turned off the lights, the room illuminated only by the soft glow of the moonlight streaming through the window.

"Goodnight, Arhan," she said softly, settling under the covers.

"Goodnight, Ammu," he replied, his heart racing in a way he couldn't explain.

After a moment's hesitation, he chose the couch instead, hoping it would help ease the tension he felt. "I'll just... sleep here for tonight."

"Are you sure?" she asked, concern lacing her voice. "I don't want you to feel uncomfortable."

"I'll be fine," he assured her, forcing a casual tone. "I just think it's better this way."

As he lay on the couch, staring up at the ceiling, he couldn't shake the feeling that this was only the beginning of something unexpected. Something that could change everything. The arrangement felt less like a contract and more like a fragile thread, just waiting to be woven into a tapestry of their lives.

And as the night wrapped around them, both of their hearts whispered promises of what could be, even if they weren't ready to admit it just yet.

Chapter 12

The First Day as a Couple

The first light of dawn crept through the window, casting a soft glow across the room. Arhan stirred awake on the couch, his body stiff from the unfamiliar position. He rubbed the sleep from his eyes and glanced around, the silence in the house almost palpable. That's when he spotted her.

Ammu was still asleep in their bed, tangled in the comforter like a butterfly caught in its cocoon. Her hair fanned out across the pillow, framing her peaceful face, and there was something utterly enchanting about the way she lay there. A stray lock had fallen across her forehead, and the sight made him chuckle softly. Despite his usual disdain for clumsiness, there was a delicate charm to her disarray, even in sleep.

He stood up, stretching out the kinks in his muscles, and walked over to the bed. The way she breathed, lips slightly parted, intrigued him. He hesitated, a strange warmth spreading through his chest as he leaned closer, unable to resist the urge to brush the hair from her face.

Just a quick adjustment, he told himself, trying to shake off the flutter of something more.

As he reached out, his fingers barely grazing her hair, Ammu stirred. "Mmm," she murmured, blinking open her eyes. A moment of confusion crossed her features before her gaze locked onto his. "Arhan?" she squeaked, panic lacing her voice as she recoiled slightly, pulling the blanket up to her chin.

He straightened, feeling his cheeks heat at the misunderstanding. "I was just—"

"Just what?" she shot back, a playful smirk creeping onto her lips. "Trying to touch my hair? I didn't know you were so romantic in the mornings!"

"What? No! I was—" he stammered, caught off guard by her teasing tone. "I was just fixing your hair."

"Fixing my hair?" she echoed, raising an eyebrow, her eyes sparkling with mischief. "Is that what they call it these days?"

"Listen, Ammu," he found his voice, the edges of his authority slipping back into place despite the awkwardness. "You're all over the place, even when you're sleeping. I thought I'd help."

"Help?" she laughed, the sound light and airy. "Or are you just trying to get a closer look at the disaster that is my morning face?"

"Disaster?" he scoffed, crossing his arms, but his heart raced at the sight of her smile. "You could have fooled me. I've seen worse disasters in board meetings."

"Ha! You mean you've seen worse disasters in your reflection," she shot back, sitting up and tossing her hair over her shoulder. "Point taken, though. I look like a raccoon right now."

He couldn't help but laugh. "There's nothing raccoon-like about you. You're just... unique."

"Unique?" she repeated, her grin widening. "Is that the new code for 'clumsy' in your world?"

"Maybe," he conceded, a teasing smile playing on his lips. "But I prefer to think of it as charming."

"Charming, huh? You're really laying it on thick this morning," she said, her voice laced with mock seriousness. "Are you trying to butter me up for something?"

"No! I just—" He rubbed the back of his neck, feeling the heat rise again. "You're cute when you're quiet. I mean, uh, when you're sleeping. It's... refreshing."

"Refreshing?" Ammu's eyes sparkled with mischief. "So you're saying I'm a little too loud when I'm awake?"

"Only when you're being a troublemaker," he shot back, unable to suppress a grin.

"Troublemaker? Me? Never!" she declared, feigning innocence. "I'm just full of surprises."

"Surprises, huh? Like tripping over your own feet during our first dance?" he teased, recalling the moment from their wedding. She had stumbled, and he had nearly lost his composure, half-wondering if it was all part of her plan.

"Hey! I was just testing your reflexes," Ammu protested, her laughter echoing through the room. "Besides, you caught me, didn't you?"

"Barely," he smirked, shaking his head. "If it weren't for my quick thinking, we'd have both been on the floor."

"Well, I appreciate your superhero skills," she said, crossing her arms and leaning back against the headboard, her smile softening. "You know, you're not as insufferable as I thought you'd be."

"Thanks, I guess," he replied, his heart fluttering at her words. "But don't let it go to your head."

"Too late!" she shot back, her eyes twinkling. "I'm already picturing myself on a throne, ruling over my kingdom of clumsiness."

"You'll need a jester for that," he retorted, raising an eyebrow. "I'm sure Vihaan would be happy to fill that role."

"Vihaan?" she exclaimed, her face scrunching up in mock disgust. "He's been banished from my kingdom!"

"Banished? That's a little harsh, don't you think?" Arhan asked, trying to keep his tone light.

"Not at all! He can be a bit... intense," she said, waving her hand dismissively. "I mean, he thought I was going to fall for his 'charming' ways. Please!"

"Charming ways? I didn't know he had any!" Arhan laughed, enjoying the playful banter. "What's the secret?"

"Just a lot of exaggerated flattery and bad puns," Ammu said, rolling her eyes. "I much prefer your approach. It's refreshing."

"Refreshing, huh?" he echoed, a hint of warmth creeping into his tone. "Maybe I should take notes."

"Definitely," she agreed, leaning forward, her expression suddenly earnest. "But only if you promise to keep being your charming self."

"Charming is my middle name," he quipped, feeling the tension ease between them.

"More like arrogant," she shot back, her eyes narrowing playfully. "But I suppose I could live with that."

"Arrogant?" he feigned shock. "I prefer 'confident.'"

"Confident, sure. Whatever helps you sleep at night, Mr. CEO," she replied, folding her arms across her chest, a teasing smile dancing on her lips.

"Now you're just making fun of me," he said, shaking his head, though his heart warmed at the light-hearted teasing.

"Maybe a little," she admitted, her laughter ringing out like music. "But it's all in good fun!"

"I'll take it," he replied, a genuine smile breaking across his face. "Just wait until I get my revenge."

"Revenge?" she gasped, clutching her heart dramatically. "What are you planning? An elaborate scheme to embarrass me?"

"Nothing so grand," he assured her, his tone casual. "Just a little payback whenever the opportunity arises."

"Bring it on!" she challenged, her eyes gleaming with excitement. "I'm ready for whatever you throw at me!"

"Are you sure?" he asked, unable to resist a playful grin. "You might just end up regretting that."

"Regretting? Never! I thrive on challenges," she declared, puffing out her chest. "I'm Ammu the Brave!"

A smile tugged at his lips as he watched her embrace her antics. "Ammu the Brave, huh? I'll have to remember that."

"Just wait until I prove it to you!" she said, her voice filled with determination. "You'll see!"

"I look forward to it," he replied, his heart racing. There was something about her spirit that captivated him, drawing him in like a moth to a flame.

As their laughter filled the room, a sense of ease enveloped them, blurring the lines of their arrangement.

In that moment, Arhan realized he was beginning to look forward to what came next. The morning sun continued to rise, casting a golden hue over their new life together, and for the first time, he felt a flicker of excitement about this unexpected journey.

"Alright, brave Ammu," he said, breaking the comfortable silence. "What's the plan for the day?"

"Operation 'Make Arhan Smile' is in full effect!" she declared, her voice brimming with enthusiasm. "And it starts with breakfast!"

"Breakfast?" he echoed, raising an eyebrow. "What exactly does that entail?"

"Just you wait and see!" she said, hopping out of bed with an uncontainable burst of energy. She nearly tripped over the blanket, but with a swift twirl, she managed to catch herself. "See? I'm a master of grace!"

"Master of grace, indeed," he chuckled, shaking his head at her antics. "You're something else, Ammu."

"I know, right?" she grinned, her eyes sparkling with mischief. "Now, go get ready while I whip up something spectacular!"

As he watched her bustle around the room, Arhan found himself shaking his head, a smile spreading across his face. Maybe this arrangement wouldn't be so bad after all. With Ammu, every day promised to be an adventure, full of laughter and surprises. And just like that, the clumsy girl had begun to weave her way into his heart in ways he hadn't anticipated.

With a newfound sense of excitement, he headed to the bathroom, ready to face whatever the day had in store for them. Little did he know, this was just the beginning of their enchanting story, one filled with love, laughter, and perhaps a little chaos—just the way Ammu liked it.

Chapter 13

A Guilt

The buzzing of the office was a familiar hum for Arhan as he strode through the sleek, modern space of his company. The walls were adorned with motivational quotes and framed achievements, a testament to his relentless drive. Today, however, the atmosphere felt different. There was a palpable energy in the air, a mischievous undertone that he couldn't quite shake off.

Kethan leaned against Arhan's desk, a teasing grin plastered across his face. "So, how was your first night as a married man?" He winked, nudging Nishan, who was trying to suppress a laugh.

Arhan rolled his eyes, crossing his arms. "It was fine, thank you very much."

"Just fine?" Nishan chimed in, barely able to contain his amusement. "Come on, don't leave us hanging! Did you two... you know?"

"Nothing happened," Arhan snapped, his voice sharper than he intended. The heat rose to his cheeks, but he quickly brushed it off. "We were busy getting to know each other."

Kethan raised an eyebrow. "Getting to know each other, huh? You're awfully defensive for a guy who was known for his 'no-strings-attached' lifestyle."

"Yeah, ever since you tied the knot, you're a different person," Nishan teased, leaning back in his chair. "Who knew marriage could change a man so quickly?"

The words hung in the air, resonating deeper than Arhan wanted to admit. He felt the weight of their jests, a flicker of doubt igniting in his mind. Was he really changing because of Ammu? The thought gnawed at him as he maintained his composure. "I'm still the same Arhan," he retorted, but the conviction in his voice failed to convince even himself.

Meanwhile, in the cozy chaos of their apartment, Ammu was on a mission. She had decided that tonight would be special; she wanted to impress Arhan with a home-cooked dinner. Armed with a cookbook and boundless enthusiasm, she whisked ingredients around the kitchen.

"Just a pinch of this... and a dash of that!" Ammu chirped, her voice echoing in the small space. Flour dusted the countertops like a light snowfall, and the scent of something burning wafted through the air.

"Uhoh," she muttered, glancing at the stovetop, where a small fire crackled menacingly. "Okay, maybe that's a little too much heat... or a lot too much!"

Ammu frantically grabbed a towel, waving it in front of the flames, but her efforts only made things worse. The smoke alarm blared, filling the room with an obnoxious wail.

"Great! Just great!" she groaned, fanning the air. "This was supposed to be a nice surprise!"

Arhan walked through the door, the scent of charred food hitting him like a brick wall. "What in the world—"

His gaze landed on the chaotic scene: flour-covered countertops, burnt pots, and Ammu standing amidst the chaos, her hair sticking out in wild directions, a mixture of panic and determination on her face.

"Ammu, what happened?" he asked, exasperation creeping into his voice.

"I was trying to cook dinner!" she exclaimed, her voice rising. "I wanted to make something special for you."

Arhan's frustration bubbled over. "This doesn't look special; it looks like a disaster! You could've set the whole place on fire!"

Ammu's eyes widened, her bright spirit dimming under his harsh words. "I... I just wanted to make you happy," she whispered, a tremor in her voice.

As silence settled, Arhan's heart sank. He watched as tears welled in her eyes, and the realization hit him like a cold wave. He had raised his voice, scared her, and for what?

The chaos was a simple mistake, an innocent attempt to make him proud.

"Ammu, I... I didn't mean to shout," he stammered, his tone softening. But she turned away, wiping at her eyes, and his guilt surged. "I'm sorry."

She paused, her back still turned to him. "Sorry doesn't fix the kitchen or how I feel right now," she said, her voice small.

It was the first time Arhan had ever apologized to anyone, and the gravity of it weighed heavily on him. "I... I know. I just—" He ran a hand through his hair, frustration boiling within him. Why did it hurt to see her upset? Why did he care so much?

He stepped closer, his heart racing as he reached out to touch her shoulder gently. "Ammu, please look at me."

Slowly, she turned, her teary eyes meeting his. "You're mad at me," she said, her voice breaking.

"No, I'm not," he replied, feeling the sincerity of his words. "I was mad at the situation. I don't want you to feel like you have to impress me. I'm... I'm still trying to figure this all out."

"Figure what out?" she asked, wiping her eyes with the back of her hand.

"Us," he admitted, the vulnerability in his voice surprising even him. "I didn't mean to take it out on you. I just... I'm not used to this. To caring about someone."

Ammu blinked, the surprise flickering in her gaze. "Oh... I didn't know you felt that way."

"Yeah," he said, his voice dropping to a softer tone. "And I don't like how it makes me feel. Like I'm changing."

"But change isn't always bad, Arhan," she said gently. "Sometimes it means you're growing. Together."

He searched her eyes, her innocence shining through despite the tears. "Together," he echoed, the weight of her words settling in his heart. "I guess I can try."

Chapter 14

Friends?

The morning sun streamed through the kitchen window, casting a warm glow over the remnants of last night's culinary disaster. Flour still clung to the countertops like a stubborn ghost, and the lingering scent of burnt toast hung heavily in the air. Ammu stood at the sink, scrubbing a charred pot with a sponge, her brow furrowed in concentration.

"Ugh! How did I manage to ruin a simple dinner?" she muttered to herself, as she scrubbed furiously, wishing the memories of last night would wash away just as easily.

Arhan entered the kitchen, his eyes narrowing at the sight. "Ammu, you know you can't just—"

"Just what?" she interjected, turning to face him with a defiant look. "Make a disaster out of your kitchen?"

He sighed, running a hand through his hair in exasperation. "I didn't mean it like that."

"Then how did you mean it?" she asked, her voice rising a notch. "You've got to understand, I'm trying here. I really am! This was supposed to be a nice surprise."

"Which turned into a fire hazard," he replied, his tone slightly softer now. "I just... I want you to be safe, Ammu."

"Safe?" she echoed, disbelief coloring her words. "You think I'm some fragile flower that needs protection? We're married, Arhan, but it's not like we're in a fairytale. This was an agreement, remember?"

The words hung in the air, thick with tension. Arhan's expression shifted, a flicker of realization passing over his features. "You're right. I just..."

"I know you're trying to be nice," she interrupted, crossing her arms over her chest. "But you don't have to feel sorry for me. I'm not a damsel in distress, and I don't need rescuing."

Silence fell between them, the only sound the soft drip of water from the sink. Arhan's brows furrowed, and he studied her face, trying to decipher the mix of determination and vulnerability reflected in her eyes. "I didn't mean to come off that way. I just— I care, Ammu."

"Care, or pity?" she asked, her voice steady but tinged with frustration. "There's a difference, you know."

"I guess I didn't think about it like that," he admitted, rubbing the back of his neck, a nervous habit he had adopted over the years. "I'm still trying to figure out how to be... well, a husband."

"Then let's start with being friends first," she suggested, her tone softening. "Can we do that? Just take it one step at a time?"

He frowned. "Friends? We're married, Ammu."

"Exactly! Which is why we should know each other better," she replied, her enthusiasm creeping back in. "Besides, I can't just keep messing up in the kitchen every time I want to impress you. It'll be easier if we're on the same team."

"On the same team, huh?" Arhan echoed, a hint of a smile breaking through his serious demeanor. "What would that even look like?"

Ammu leaned against the sink, her playful side surfacing. "Well, for starters, you could help me with cooking lessons. You know, teach me how not to burn down the house!"

Arhan chuckled, the sound surprising even him. "I'm not sure I'm the best teacher when it comes to that."

"Come on! I'll bring the enthusiasm, and you bring the 'don't burn your hand on the stove' advice!" She grinned, her energy infectious. "We can even make it fun. Maybe turn it into a cooking competition!"

"Competition?" he raised an eyebrow, intrigued. "Against you? I think I'd win that one hands down."

"Challenge accepted!" Ammu shot back, her laughter ringing in the small kitchen, brightening the grim atmosphere.

"I'll make sure to keep the fire extinguisher close," he teased, crossing his arms, fully leaning into her playful spirit.

They shared a moment of easy laughter, the tension gradually melting away. But beneath the light-hearted banter, Arhan couldn't shake the thought of their situation. "Ammu, I just don't want you to think you have to impress me. You don't need to prove anything."

"Maybe not," she said, her voice quieter now. "But I want to be someone you would want to know, not just some girl you're married to because of an agreement."

The sincerity in her words struck him, and for a moment, he was speechless. "You're more than that to me, Ammu," he finally managed to say. "I didn't realize how much I needed to change my perspective. It's just... everything is new."

"New can be exciting," she encouraged, her eyes sparkling. "Think of it as an adventure. We get to create our own rules, our own memories."

"Memories, huh?" he mused, the corners of his mouth twitching upward. "Like the memory of you almost burning my kitchen down?"

"Exactly!" she laughed, her eyes gleaming with mischief. "And now we can add 'cooking lessons' to the list of things we can do together."

Arhan stepped closer, the kitchen suddenly feeling smaller, more intimate. "Okay, but if we do this, I want to know you better too. No more hiding behind clumsiness or childishness. I want the real Ammu."

"Deal!" she exclaimed, her smile radiating warmth. "But you've got to promise to be patient with me. I'm not perfect."

"I wouldn't want you to be," he replied, his voice low and sincere. "That's what makes you... you."

Ammu felt a flutter in her stomach, a warmth spreading through her at his words. "So, friends?"

"Friends," he confirmed, extending his hand toward her.

She took it, their hands fitting together naturally, and for the first time, the agreement felt less like a contract and more like a promise.

"Okay," she said, pulling her hand back with a grin. "What's first on the agenda for our friendship? A cooking lesson or a trip to the market? I hear the fresh produce is to die for!"

"Let's start with the market," he suggested, the thought of venturing out into the vibrant streets of Mumbai alongside her igniting a spark of excitement. "I want to see your clumsiness in action."

"Clumsiness in action?" she replied with a mock gasp. "You're going to regret that statement when I trip over my own two feet!"

"Maybe I'll catch you," he said, a teasing glint in his eyes.

"Or maybe you'll just laugh at me," she countered, sticking her tongue out playfully.

"Definitely a little of both," he admitted, amusement dancing in his gaze. "But I'll always be here to help you up."

Ammu hesitated for a moment, her heart pounding at the sincerity in his voice. "You really mean that?"

"Of course," he nodded firmly. "I may not be a perfect husband yet, but I can at least be a good friend."

"Good! Because that's all I really need right now," she said, her voice lightening. "And who knows? Maybe we'll discover that we're better together than apart."

As they exchanged smiles, the tension of their marriage began to dissolve, replaced by a budding friendship that promised laughter, support, and a sprinkling of chaos.

"Let's go, then!" Ammu declared, grabbing her bag with renewed energy. "But I need to make sure I don't leave a mess behind this time. I'll be right back!"

Arhan watched as she dashed out of the kitchen, her laughter trailing behind her like a melody. He shook his head, a smile creeping onto his face. Maybe this wouldn't be so bad after all.

As he took a moment to appreciate the mess surrounding him, he realized that where there was chaos, there was also life. And in this new chapter, he was ready to embrace every clumsy, chaotic moment with Ammu by his side.

Chapter 15

The Pub

The neon lights of the pub flickered like the stars that Ammu had always dreamed of dancing under. The thumping bass resonated through her chest, and the atmosphere buzzed with laughter and energy. She spun around, her arms flaring out as she twirled on the dance floor, her heart light. Ananya joined her, a whirlwind of excitement, their laughter intertwining seamlessly with the music.

"Come on, Ammu! Show me those moves!" Ananya shouted over the music, her eyes sparkling with mischief.

"Like this?" Ammu replied, attempting a clumsy spin that sent her nearly tumbling into a nearby table. She caught herself just in time, a giggle escaping her lips. "Oops!"

Kethan leaned against the bar, his gaze fixed on Priya, who was trying her best to remain unfazed by his flirtations. He flashed a charming grin. "You know, Priya, I think we could make a great team. You with your brains, and me with my... well, everything else."

Priya raised an eyebrow, unimpressed. "Is that so? And what exactly do you bring to the table besides your charming smile?"

"Charming smiles are pretty valuable, you know," Kethan replied, feigning seriousness. "Plus, I make an excellent cocktail."

Nishan, leaning next to Kethan, chuckled. "That's the only thing you're good at. Just stick to pouring drinks, Kethan."

As the DJ dropped the beat, Ammu and Ananya danced like nobody was watching, lost in their own world of laughter and joy. Ammu felt free, her worries about being a "contract wife" temporarily forgotten. She twirled, feeling the rhythm pulse through her veins, until her eyes wandered to where Arhan stood, stoic and handsome, sipping his drink. He surveyed the room with an intensity that made her heart flutter.

"Arhan!" she called, her voice cutting through the music. She stumbled toward him, a grin plastered on her face. "Come join us!"

He shook his head, a bemused smile tugging at the corners of his lips. "I'm good, Ammu. You keep having fun."

Just then, a guy from across the bar caught Ammu's eye. He was tall, with a slick hairstyle and an overconfident swagger. She watched as he approached, a smirk plastered on his face. "Hey there, pretty lady," he said, leaning closer than she was comfortable with. "Why don't you ditch your friends and dance with me?"

Ammu stepped back, her smile fading. "No, thank you. I'm fine with my friends."

"Oh, come on," he insisted, invading her personal space. "Don't be like that. You know you want to."

Arhan's demeanor shifted instantly. He narrowed his eyes, recognizing the tension from across the room. Ammu's laughter was replaced by discomfort, and that alone ignited a fire within him.

"Hey!" Ammu protested, trying to push him away gently. "I said no!"

But the guy just laughed, grabbing her wrist with a grip that made her flinch. "What's the matter? You scared?"

Before Ammu could react, Arhan was on the move. He pushed through the crowd, fury etched across his face. "How dare you touch my wife!" he shouted, his voice booming.

The guy barely had time to register the threat before Arhan's fist connected with his jaw, sending him staggering back. The pub fell silent for a split second as everyone turned to watch, the music fading into the background.

"Arhan, wait!" Ammu called, but her plea was drowned out by the chaos.

Arhan was relentless, his fists flying as he rained punches down on the guy, who was now on the floor, blood trickling from his nose. "You think you can just grab her? You think she's some toy for you to play with?" Each word was punctuated by another strike, each one fueled by rage and protectiveness.

Ammu's heart raced, a mix of fear and exhilaration swirling within her. She'd never seen this side of Arhan before, and it made her feel... special? But then the reality hit her. "I'm just a contract wife," she whispered to herself, confusion clouding her happiness.

The guy groaned, attempting to shield himself from Arhan's onslaught. "I didn't mean—"

"Shut up!" Arhan bellowed, his voice cutting through the air. "You're going to regret ever laying a finger on her!"

Ammu's eyes widened as she rushed forward, her heart pounding. "Arhan, stop! Please!" She wrapped her arms around him from behind, her presence grounding him. "You don't have to do this!"

The moment her warmth enveloped him, Arhan froze, his fists hovering inches from the guy's face. He turned slightly, his expression softening as he looked at Ammu. "But he—"

"I know!" she interjected, squeezing him tighter. "But this isn't you! Please, just let it go."

His breath was heavy, the tension radiating from his frame slowly dissipating as he took in her words. With a reluctant sigh, he stepped back, allowing the guy to scramble away, clutching his face.

"Get out of here," Arhan warned, his voice low and dangerous. The guy didn't need to be told twice; he scrambled to his feet and bolted from the pub, leaving a trail of whispers and stunned faces in his wake.

Ammu turned to Arhan, her heart racing. "You didn't have to go that far," she said, her voice trembling slightly. "I appreciate that you wanted to protect me, but..."

"But what?" he asked, an edge still present in his tone. "You think I overreacted?"

She hesitated, searching his eyes for understanding. "I'm grateful, really," she insisted, her hands trembling as she reached up to touch his arm. "But I'm not your real wife. I'm just... your contract wife."

His gaze darkened, a storm brewing behind his eyes. "What does that matter? You're my wife in every way that counts."

Ammu stepped back, her heart sinking. "But I don't want you to act like that for me, Arhan. I don't want expectations that can't be met."

He opened his mouth to argue, but the hurt in her eyes silenced him. Instead, he ran a hand through his hair, frustration bubbling beneath the surface. "You're not just a contract to me, Ammu."

"I'm sorry," she said, her voice barely above a whisper. "I just don't want to get hurt. I don't want to feel like I'm living a lie."

In that moment, the weight of their situation hung heavily in the air. Arhan turned away, unable to articulate the turmoil within him. The laughter and music of the pub faded into the background, leaving only their unresolved tension in its wake.

Ammu watched him, her heart aching. "Arhan, please just talk to me."

But he remained silent, his jaw clenched. The raw emotion swirling in the air felt too heavy to bear.

Finally, he sighed, looking back at her with a mix of frustration and longing. "I don't know how to do this," he admitted, his voice laced with vulnerability. "I've never cared about anyone like this before."

Ammu stepped forward, her heart softening at his admission. "Maybe that's okay. We're both learning. Together."

He nodded slowly, but the shadows in his eyes remained. "You deserve more than what I can give you right now."

Ammu's chest tightened. "I'm not asking for perfection, Arhan. I just want honesty. And if that means being just a contract wife, then so be it. But I need you to be real with me."

His gaze softened, the tension easing slightly. "Ammu…"

Kethan's voice cut through the moment as he approached, a concerned expression on his face. "Everything okay, guys?"

Ammu turned, forcing a smile. "Yeah, just a little… misunderstanding."

Nishan joined them, his eyes darting from Ammu to Arhan. "You sure about that? Because you both look like you've just been through a boxing match."

Arhan shot Kethan a warning glare, his emotions still tumultuous. "I'm fine."

"Right," Nishan said, clearly unconvinced. "You just took care of some guy who had it coming. But maybe we should lighten the mood? How about a round of drinks?"

Ammu glanced at Arhan, hoping he'd agree. "That sounds good, doesn't it?"

He hesitated, the internal struggle evident in his expression. Finally, he nodded, though his eyes remained distant. "Sure, drinks it is."

As they made their way back to the bar, Kethan threw an arm around Priya, who rolled her eyes but couldn't suppress a smile. "Come on, let's celebrate our survival from that disaster."

Ammu fell into step beside Arhan, her heart still heavy but hopeful. "You know," she said softly, "I didn't mean what I said about being a contract wife. I just... I don't want to fall for you and then have you pull away."

He glanced at her, his expression unreadable. "Ammu, I'm still trying to figure out what this means for us. But I promise I'm not going anywhere."

The sincerity in his voice warmed her heart, and for the first time that night, she felt the tension lift. Perhaps they could navigate this together, even if the path was uncertain.

"Together, then," she whispered, a small smile breaking through.

"Together," he echoed, a hint of a smile tugging at his lips as well.

As they settled around the bar, drinks in hand, laughter bubbled up again. The music resumed its infectious beat, and Ammu felt the warmth of friendship and newfound hope encircle her. Maybe, just maybe, they could make this work—one step at a time.

Chapter 16

Jealous Arhan

The sun peeked through the curtains, illuminating the room with a soft glow. Arhan lay in bed, staring at the ceiling, lost in thought. It was strange, this feeling that had begun to creep in since his marriage to Ammu. He had always been a man of control, his life a carefully crafted plan. Yet now, he found himself wondering about clumsy little things—like how she always managed to spill her coffee or trip over her own feet.

He rolled over, grabbing his phone and dialing Nishan's number. The line rang twice before his friend picked up, his voice cheerful and teasing. "What's up, Arhan? Calling to thank me for being the world's best wingman?"

"Very funny," Arhan muttered, propping himself up on one elbow. "I need to talk. It's... about Ammu."

"Ah, the clumsy bride! What's the matter? Did she burn down your kitchen again?" Nishan laughed, but Arhan could hear the underlying worry in his tone.

"No. It's not that. I think I'm... starting to like her." The admission slipped out before he could stop it, and he felt a flush of heat rise to his cheeks.

"Whoa! Someone's feeling mushy!" Nishan's laughter echoed through the phone. "What's the big deal? You're married. You're supposed to like her."

"Yeah, but it's different. I don't know how to express it. I've never felt this way about anyone." Arhan's voice dropped, a hint of frustration creeping in. "I'm not good at this."

"Listen, man. You've got to communicate. How can you expect her to know you're feeling all warm and fuzzy inside if you don't say anything? Women can't read minds, you know."

"Tell me about it," Arhan sighed, glancing out the window at the bustling city below. "I just don't want to scare her off."

"Scare her off? You? You're the CEO of a major company! You're intimidating even when you're trying to be nice. Just be honest, Arhan. That's all it takes."

"Easy for you to say. You've got a way with women," Arhan grumbled, his mind racing with thoughts of Ammu.

"Yeah, and look where that got me—surrounded by ex-girlfriends who still want a piece of me," Nishan joked, but his voice turned serious. "Just remember, she's not like the others. You've got to treat her differently."

"I know. She's... special." The word felt foreign on his tongue, yet it rang true. "I just don't know how to show it."

"Start by being her friend. You've already made progress! You laughed together, right?"

"Yeah, but... I don't want to be just friends," Arhan admitted, his heart racing at the realization. "I want more."

"Then go for it! Just don't let her see you sweat. Women love a man with confidence." Nishan's laughter faded, replaced by a thoughtful pause. "But hey, what's going on with you guys today?"

"Nothing. Just... the usual." Arhan's thoughts shifted as he remembered the plans he had overheard the day before. "Wait, what time is it?"

"Almost noon. Why?"

"Crap! Ammu said something about meeting Ananya and Vihaan today."

"Vihaan? Oh boy, I see where this is going," Nishan replied, a hint of laughter in his voice. "You getting jealous, Arhan?"

"No! Well, maybe a little," he stammered, running a hand through his hair. "I don't like the idea of her being with him."

"Then do something about it! Are you really going to let her go out with him without a fight?"

Arhan paused, weighing his options. "What if I pretend to be sick? That way, she'll stay home."

"Dude, that's... genius." Nishan chuckled. "Just make sure you don't overdo it. You don't want her thinking you're faking."

"Right." Arhan hung up, his heart racing. He could do this. He would keep her close, if only for a little while longer.

Ammu was humming as she moved around the house, her excitement palpable. She had just finished dressing when her phone rang. It was Ananya, her voice bright and cheerful. "Ammu! Are you ready for our girls' day out?"

"Absolutely! I can't wait to see you!" Ammu exclaimed, her heart skipping a beat at the thought of a fun day with her best friend.

"Vihaan's coming too, by the way. I hope that's okay," Ananya added, her tone teasing.

Ammu's heart fluttered at the mention of Vihaan, her childhood friend. He had always been there, always supportive, but she had never thought of him that way—at least not until now. "Oh! That's fine. Just a casual hangout, right?"

"Right! Just us friends having a great time. I'll pick you up in half an hour!"

"Perfect! I'll be ready!" Ammu hung up, her mind buzzing with thoughts of the day ahead. She rushed to find something to wear, excitement bubbling inside her.

Just as she was about to head out, she found Arhan leaning against the doorframe, looking unusually pale and tired. "Hey, are you feeling okay?" she asked, her brow furrowing in concern.

"Uh, not really," he said, trying to sound convincing. "I think I might be coming down with something."

"Oh no! What's wrong?" Ammu rushed to his side, her worries eclipsing her plans. "You should have told me sooner! Do you need anything? Soup? Medicine?"

"I think just some... rest." He coughed lightly, trying to sound pitiful. "You don't need to worry about me. You should go out with Ananya and Vihaan."

"Are you kidding? I can't leave you like this!" Ammu placed a hand on his forehead, her expression turning serious. "You're burning up! I can't let you suffer alone."

"Ammu, really, I'll be fine," he insisted, but the look in her eyes made him falter. She was sweet, and her concern was genuine.

"No, you're not. I'm staying right here to take care of you," she announced, her voice firm. "Cancel your plans and let me help."

Arhan's heart raced. "You really don't have to."

"Too late! I already decided," she said, her tone playful yet resolute. "Now, let's get you some water and some blankets. You need to rest."

As she bustled about the room, gathering supplies, Arhan couldn't help but marvel at how easily she shifted her focus from her own plans to caring for him. It was endearing and maddening all at once. "Ammu, are you sure you don't want to go? I won't hold it against you."

"Not a chance!" she replied, her voice brightening as she returned with a glass of water. "You're my husband now, and that comes with responsibilities. Like taking care of you when you're sick! So, drink up, mister."

He took the glass from her, their fingers brushing lightly. "You know, I was just going to say that I might be feeling better soon..."

"Liar!" she laughed, her eyes sparkling with mischief. "Drink your water, and I'll make you some toast."

Arhan watched her as she flitted around the room, her energy infectious. He had planned to keep her close by pretending to be ill, but as he observed her, he realized that he was genuinely enjoying her company. Maybe he didn't need to pretend anymore. Perhaps he could just let the day unfold and see where it led.

"Okay, how about this," he said, his voice steady. "If I promise to get better, will you promise to make me your famous toast?"

"I don't know if it's famous, but I can sure try," she grinned, her playful spirit shining through. "But only if you promise to let me take care of you today."

"Deal," he replied, feeling a warmth spread through him. It wasn't the day he had envisioned, but it felt right. "But remember, I might need some serious pampering."

"Oh, don't you worry!" Ammu clapped her hands, her laughter filling the room. "I'll make sure you're pampered like the king you are!"

As she dove into the kitchen, humming a cheerful tune, Arhan felt a shift within himself. The jealousy that had surged at the thought of Ammu spending time with Vihaan faded away. He realized that he wanted to be the man who could make her laugh, the one who could sweep her off her feet—not just the guy who watched her from the sidelines.

With a newfound determination, he settled in for the day, ready to embrace whatever came next. Perhaps, just perhaps, he could figure out how to express what he felt for her—one clumsy moment at a time.

Chapter 17

Mr. CEO and Clumsy Princess

The afternoon sun draped the room in a warm glow, casting playful shadows as Ammu bustled around, checking on Arhan. He lay on the couch, feigning a cough that sounded more dramatic than genuine. She paused, hands on her hips, her brow furrowed in concern.

"Aren't you being a bit... extra?" Ammu asked, tilting her head as she scrutinized him. "You know, I've seen you in meetings where you looked much worse than this. You could pass for a superhero with how you're acting."

Arhan cracked a smile, but quickly masked it with another cough. "It's a serious condition! I might—"

"Please, you're just pretending!" Ammu interrupted, her laughter bubbling up like a fizzy drink. "You didn't even have the decency to act sick while I was making toast. You just lounged there, looking like a model from a magazine."

He couldn't help but chuckle at her unfiltered commentary. "Okay, maybe I overdid it a little."

"Just a little?" Ammu rolled her eyes, crossing her arms playfully. "Arhan, you're the worst actor I've ever seen. What's going on? Why would you pretend to be sick?"

He hesitated, the weight of his confession pressing on him like a heavy blanket. "I... I didn't want you to go out with Ananya and Vihaan."

Ammu blinked, her surprise evident. "Really? You went through all this trouble just for that? You know you could've just asked me to stay home, right?"

"I know," he said, running a hand through his hair, a nervous habit he had yet to shake. "But I didn't want you to think I was being controlling or something. It just... it felt easier this way."

"Easier?" she echoed, her voice rising in disbelief. "Lying is easier than just being honest?"

He sighed, the weight of his emotions crashing over him. "Ammu, there's something you need to know."

"What is it?" she asked, her tone shifting to one of genuine curiosity.

"I'm not the same person I was before. I feel... different. Since we got married, I've started to change. I'm not just the corporate machine I used to be. I'm... starting to fall for you."

Ammu's eyes widened, and her heart raced. "What? You're falling for me?" The words tumbled out, almost breathless, as she processed the confession. "Like, really? You mean it?"

"Completely. Your innocence, your clumsiness, it's all so... refreshing. I never thought I could feel this way about anyone." His voice softened, vulnerability threading through his words. "But you make me want to be better."

Ammu's heart soared. She felt like she had stepped into one of the romantic dramas she loved. Her fingers danced in excitement, and without thinking, she jumped up and down, her laughter echoing through the room. "Oh my gosh! This is like a fairytale! I can't believe you, Arhan!"

He watched her, a mixture of relief and disbelief flooding him. "You're not mad?"

"Mad? Are you kidding?" She beamed, her eyes sparkling with delight. "This is amazing! I'm going to have my own fairytale with my husband!"

"Wait, so you're okay with this? With me?" he asked, astonished by her reaction.

"Of course! But..." she paused, biting her lip as a mischievous grin spread across her face. "If we're going to do this whole love thing, you have to promise to pamper me. You know, like they do in K-dramas!"

Arhan raised an eyebrow, half-expecting her to burst out laughing. "Pamper you? You mean like... holding your hand while we watch movies? Or running around in the rain?"

"Yes! Exactly!" Ammu clapped her hands, bouncing on her toes. "And surprise kisses! And romantic dinners! And maybe even a dance in the rain!"

He chuckled, the idea of dancing in the rain was absurd, yet the thought of Ammu's joy made his heart swell. "Okay, I'll try to be the man you imagined. But you have to promise not to trip over your own feet during the dance."

"Hey!" She playfully shoved his shoulder, her laughter infectious. "I may be clumsy, but I can dance! Just you wait!"

"I look forward to it," he said, a smile spreading across his face. "But for now, how about you help me get better?"

Ammu's eyes sparkled with mischief. "Only if you promise to take me on a date tonight. I want to dress up and be spoiled!"

"Deal," he replied, feeling lighter than he had in a long time. "I'll do my best to treat you like a queen."

"Yay!" She squealed, clapping her hands again. "I can't wait! We'll make it a night to remember, Arhan!"

As Ammu flitted around the room, gathering supplies to make him soup, Arhan couldn't help but marvel at the shift in their relationship. The tension that had hung between them was dissipating, replaced by a warmth he hadn't anticipated. She was the sunshine in his carefully constructed world, and he was more than willing to let her in.

"Just promise me one thing," he said, his tone turning serious.

"Anything!" Ammu chirped, her back turned as she rummaged through the kitchen.

"Promise me you'll always be yourself. I don't want you to change, even if I'm trying to be better."

Ammu paused, glancing over her shoulder with a soft smile. "I promise, Arhan. I'll always be your clumsy little Ammu. And you'll always be my handsome CEO."

"Sounds like a plan," he said, feeling a sense of hope that he hadn't felt in years.

As the scents of soup wafted through the air, Arhan's heart raced with anticipation. Tonight would be different; it would be the first of many steps into a world where they could explore their feelings together.

"Okay, Mr. CEO," Ammu announced, her voice sing-songy as she placed a steaming bowl in front of him. "Eat up! You need your strength for our K-drama date later."

He chuckled, the sound bubbling up from his chest. "What if I'm too sick to eat?"

"Not a chance!" Ammu pointed a wooden spoon at him, her eyes twinkling with determination. "You're going to eat like a king. Besides, I'm not letting you off that easy."

As he took a spoonful of the soup, warmth spread through him, not just from the food, but from the realization that he was finally opening up to someone who truly understood him. Ammu was his breath of fresh air, and he would do everything in his power to cherish her.

"So, what's first on our list for the date?" he asked, savoring the taste as she sat beside him, her eager presence brightening his mood.

"First, we'll watch a romantic movie! Then, we can recreate a scene from it! Maybe the part where the leads kiss under the stars?" Ammu suggested, her eyes glimmering with excitement.

"And what if it rains?" he teased, a smirk playing on his lips.

"Then we'll dance in it! Right in the middle of the street, like true stars!" Ammu exclaimed, her enthusiasm spilling over.

Arhan couldn't help but laugh, the image of them twirling under the raindrops making his heart race. "You're going to be the death of me, you know that?"

"And you're going to be the best thing that ever happened to me!" she shot back, beaming.

As the afternoon slipped into evening, they shared stories, laughter, and a connection that deepened with every passing moment. For the first time, Arhan felt like he was living—not just existing in a world of meetings and deadlines, but truly living, filled with joy and the promise of love.

"Alright, you win," he said finally, looking into her eyes with sincerity. "I'll try to fulfill your K-drama dreams. But you have to remember, I'm still learning how to be this... romantic guy."

"Don't worry! You'll be amazing!" Ammu said, her voice brimming with confidence. "This is just the beginning of our adventure, Arhan."

And with that, Arhan knew he would do everything to make it a story worth telling—a fairytale that was distinctly theirs, filled with clumsiness, laughter, and a love that could withstand anything.

Chapter 18

Little Romance

The evening wrapped around their home like a cozy blanket, the soft glow of the lamps casting warm pools of light across the living room. Arhan shifted on the couch, the awkwardness in the air palpable. He stole glances at Ammu, who was sitting across from him, her fingers nervously twisting the edge of her sweater. They were no longer just an arranged couple—now, they were Arhan and Ammu, bound together not only by their families but by a budding romance that had taken root in the most unexpected of circumstances.

"Um, so... what's next on our K-drama adventure?" Ammu asked, her voice a mix of eagerness and uncertainty. She was trying to play it cool, but her eyes betrayed her excitement.

Arhan swallowed hard, his heart racing. "Well, we could start with... uh, I don't know, some romantic music?" His voice felt foreign, heavy with the weight of what was about to happen.

"Music sounds good!" she exclaimed, her smile brightening the dim room. But then her expression shifted, an adorable furrow forming in her brow. "But what if it's just too... much?"

He chuckled, trying to ease the tension. "Too much? Ammu, you're the one who wanted to recreate a movie scene! This is like our first romantic date as a real couple."

"Right! But still..." She hesitated, biting her lip, the very picture of sweet innocence that both thrilled and terrified him.

"Are you... scared?" he asked, leaning a little closer, heart pounding. "Because I can stop if you want."

Ammu's eyes darted away, her cheeks flushing a shade of pink that made him want to reach out and brush the color across her face. "It's not that I don't want to... it's just. I've never really done this before," she admitted, her voice barely above a whisper.

"Neither have I," he confessed, the admission slipping out before he could catch it. "But I want to. With you."

"Okay," she said, her voice stronger now, but her gaze remained fixed on her lap. "But, um... can you give me some time?"

"Time?" The word hung between them, a fragile bridge over a chasm of unspoken feelings. "How much time?"

"Just... a little," she replied, glancing up at him, her eyes wide and earnest. "I promise, I want this too. I just... need to breathe."

Arhan nodded, pulling back slightly, trying to respect her request and the boundaries they were still learning to navigate. He felt like a tightrope walker, balancing between ambition and caution, yearning and restraint. "Okay, I can do that. Just... don't take too long."

She laughed nervously, the sound like a melody that eased some of the tension. "I'll try not to."

"Great. I'll, um, go take a shower then," he stammered, standing up awkwardly. The warm glow of the living room felt too intimate, too charged. He needed to cool off, to clear his head.

"Yeah, good idea!" she chirped, a bit too enthusiastically.

As he walked toward the bathroom, he could feel her gaze burning into his back. The door clicked shut behind him, and he leaned against it for a moment, taking a deep breath. The cool tiles of the bathroom were a welcome contrast to the heat swirling around him. He turned on the shower, letting the water cascade down his body, hoping it would quell the wild emotions that surged within him.

But even as he rinsed away the remnants of the day, thoughts of Ammu swirled in his mind. Her laughter, her innocence, the way her eyes sparkled when she was excited—it was intoxicating. And yet, the fear of crossing that line loomed large. What if he scared her off? What if she wasn't ready for what he felt?

After a long, indulgent shower, he stepped out, the steam enveloping him in a warm embrace. He reached for a towel, wrapping it around his waist, and caught a glimpse of himself in the mirror. Water dripped down his chest, and he ran a hand through his damp hair, trying to shake off the lingering doubts.

With a sigh, he opened the bathroom door, feeling lighter yet somehow more exposed. As he stepped back into the living room, he found Ammu sitting on the couch, her eyes wide as they landed on him.

"Uh," she stammered, her cheeks turning an even deeper shade of crimson. "You... um, you look... nice?"

"Nice?" he echoed, a smirk creeping onto his lips. "Is that all you can come up with? I'm practically—"

"Shhh!" she interrupted, her voice a frantic whisper. "You're just... a lot to take in right now!"

He chuckled, his heart racing at her flustered state. "Ammu, it's just a towel."

"Yes, but—" She gestured wildly, her hands flying as if trying to create a barrier between them. "You're not wearing anything else!"

"True." He leaned against the doorframe, enjoying her reaction. "But you're the one who said you needed time for romance. I thought maybe you'd like to see the full package."

"Arhan!" she squeaked, burying her face in her hands, and he couldn't help but burst into laughter at her embarrassment.

"Okay, okay, I'll behave." He stepped closer, the towel clinging to his waist, the air thickening with unspoken words and possibilities. "But seriously, Ammu, you're safe with me. I promise I won't rush you."

Her eyes peeked out from behind her fingers, and he could see the mix of shyness and curiosity dancing within them. "I know," she murmured, dropping her hands and meeting his gaze. "It's just... new. And I don't want to mess it up."

"It's okay to be scared," he said softly, his heart aching for her. "But I'm here. We're in this together."

Ammu took a deep breath, her expression shifting from embarrassment to determination. "Okay," she said, her voice steadier now. "Let's take it slow. Together."

"Together," he echoed, the word wrapping around them like a promise. He stepped closer, the distance between them shrinking, his heart racing as he leaned in. The warmth from the towel, the softness of her hair, everything felt electric.

But then, he paused, hovering just inches from her. "Can I...?" he asked, his voice low and hesitant, seeking her permission.

She looked up at him, her eyes wide with vulnerability, but there was a flicker of something deeper there—trust. "Yes," she whispered, her breath hitching. "You can."

In that moment, all the tension, the fear, the uncertainty melted away. He closed the gap, his lips brushing against hers, a gentle exploration filled with warmth and promise. It started softly, a sweet caress that sent shivers down his spine. As he leaned in more, feeling the softness of her lips against his, it was as if the world around them faded into nothingness.

Ammu responded shyly at first, her lips barely moving against his, but as he deepened the kiss, she melted into him. He could feel her warmth radiating, wrapping around him like a cocoon, and their hearts beat in synchrony.

When they finally pulled away, their foreheads resting against each other, he could see the confusion and excitement swirling in her eyes. "Wow," she breathed, a smile breaking across her face. "That was... different."

"Different good?" he asked, his heart racing.

"Definitely good," she replied, her laughter bubbling up, filling the room with a lightness that made him grin. "I think I could get used to this."

"Me too," he said, feeling a rush of exhilaration. "I think we're onto something here."

"Just promise me one thing," Ammu said, her expression turning serious again.

"What's that?"

"Promise we'll take it one step at a time, and you won't turn into a total CEO monster on me." She giggled, and he couldn't help but join her, the sound echoing around them.

"Deal," he replied, a sense of relief washing over him. "As long as you promise to keep being my clumsy, wonderful Ammu."

"Always," she said, her eyes sparkling with mischief. "And next time, maybe wear a little more than just a towel?"

"Only if you promise to wear something equally distracting," he shot back, his playful grin returning.

She laughed, a bright sound that filled the room with warmth, and in that moment, Arhan knew they were just beginning. A new chapter awaited them, and he was ready to embrace it all—clumsiness, laughter, and the beautiful chaos of love.

Chapter 19

Vihaan's Confession

The sun dipped low over Mumbai, casting a golden hue across the bustling streets as Ammu and Arhan settled into their routine at the office. The atmosphere buzzed with the energy of an impending meeting, but Ammu seemed lost in a world of her own, daydreaming about their last evening together.

"Hey, Ammu! Earth to Ammu!" Ananya's teasing voice broke through her reverie.

"Hmm?" Ammu blinked, shaking her head as if waking from a pleasant dream. "Oh, sorry! Just thinking about... um, work! Yeah, work."

Ananya raised an eyebrow, clearly unconvinced. "Work? Or Arhan? Come on, spill the tea! How's the married life treating you?"

Ammu's cheeks flushed. "It's... it's great! He's really sweet, you know? Like, he actually laughs at my jokes."

"Wow, that's a miracle!" Ananya giggled, leaning closer. "But seriously, you're glowing! I think you've been bitten by the love bug."

Before Ammu could respond, Vihaan appeared at the door, his expression a mix of determination and anxiety. "Ammu, can we talk?"

"Um, sure," Ammu replied, a hint of apprehension creeping into her voice. She stood up, glancing at Ananya, who watched with wide eyes.

Vihaan led her to a quieter corner of the office, away from prying ears. "Ammu, I need to tell you something important."

"What's wrong?" she asked, her brow furrowing.

"It's about your marriage with Arhan," he said, his voice low. "I know it's an arranged one, and I... I can't keep quiet any longer."

Ammu felt her heart race. "What do you mean?"

"I mean, I've always had feelings for you. I thought maybe... maybe we could give it a try. You and me. I could make you happier than he ever could."

Ammu's eyes widened in shock. "Vihaan, I—"

"Just hear me out!" he interrupted, desperation etching his features. "I care about you. You deserve someone who sees you for who you are, not just as a business deal."

"It's not like that!" Ammu protested, her voice rising. "We're happy together. Arhan is—he's amazing! I love him!"

Vihaan clenched his fists, frustration bubbling beneath the surface. "You think he loves you? This is just a contract to him! You're just fulfilling a duty."

"Stop!" she shouted, her heart pounding. "You don't know what you're talking about. Love isn't a contract! It's real, and he cares for me!"

"Cares for you?" he scoffed. "What kind of love is that? You're a pawn in this game!"

Ammu took a step back, her heart aching. "I'm not a pawn! I chose this. I chose him."

Vihaan's expression softened for a moment, but he quickly masked it with a forced smile. "If it's really love, then why don't you tell Priya? She deserves to know about the agreement."

"Why would I tell her that?" Ammu felt a chill run down her spine. "It's not her business."

"It is if you're serious about Arhan," he insisted. "What happens when she finds out? You think she'll just sit back and watch you get hurt?"

"Vihaan, please…" Ammu's voice trembled.

"I just want you to be happy, Ammu," he said, his tone shifting. "But if you're really in love, then you'll tell Priya and face the truth."

Ammu shook her head, unable to process his words. "I need to go."

As she turned away, Vihaan called after her, "Just think about it, Ammu! Please!"

* * *

Later that day, Ammu found herself at a café with Priya. They clinked their cups together, the sound ringing lightly in the air.

"Cheers to my amazing sister!" Priya said, her smile bright. "I can't believe you're married! How does it feel?"

"It feels... wonderful," Ammu replied, her heart heavy with uncertainty.

"Good! But you know, I heard some rumors about Arhan and his past. I want to make sure he treats you right."

Ammu's stomach twisted. "What kind of rumors?"

"Just stuff about him being cold and distant. I mean, he's a CEO, right? A serious guy?" Priya shrugged. "I just want you to be careful."

"I can take care of myself!" Ammu snapped, the tension between them palpable. "You don't have to worry about me."

"Fine, fine! Just looking out for you," Priya said, holding up her hands in mock surrender. "But if you ever need to talk—"

Before she could finish, Ammu's phone buzzed. It was a message from Kethan, Arhan's secretary.

"Hey, Ammu. Can you meet me? I need to discuss something important about Arhan."

Ammu's heart raced at the urgency in his words. She glanced at Priya. "I have to go. Kethan needs me."

"Okay, but—"

"I'll call you later!" Ammu interrupted, already rising from her seat.

As she hurried out of the café, her mind raced. What could Kethan want to discuss? Was it about the agreement? Her heart sank at the thought of what might happen if Arhan's past came to light.

* * *

Meanwhile, Priya pulled out her phone, a frown settling on her face as she dialed Kethan's number. "Hey, Kethan, it's Priya. I need to ask you something. It's about Ammu and Arhan... it's serious."

"Yeah?" Kethan replied, his voice steady.

"I heard something about their marriage being an agreement. Can you confirm this?"

Silence hung heavily in the air as Priya waited for an answer.

"Priya, it's not what you think…"

"Then what is it? I need to know!"

Kethan sighed deeply. "I can't say much, but… Ammu and Arhan did marry under certain conditions. But it's complicated."

"Complicated how?" Priya pressed, her heart racing. "You need to tell me everything."

As Kethan hesitated, Priya felt a wave of determination wash over her. She had to protect her sister, no matter what it took.

"Just meet me," Kethan finally said. "We need to talk."

Priya nodded, a new sense of urgency igniting within her. "I'll be there."

As she hung up, she knew this was just the beginning. The truth about Ammu and Arhan's marriage was about to unfold, and she would do everything in her power to protect her sister from any pain that might come their way.

Chapter 20

A Feel of Betrayal

The sun hung low in the sky, casting long shadows across the polished floors of Arhan's office. Kethan sat behind the imposing mahogany desk, his fingers tapping nervously against the surface. The weight of the world felt heavier today, especially with Priya pacing in front of him, her expression a mix of concern and determination.

"Kethan, I need you to understand," Priya said, her voice steady but urgent. "This isn't just about Ammu and Arhan. It's about their future, and I can't let her get hurt."

Kethan clenched his jaw. "You think I don't know that? But you're asking me to betray my brother. You're saying he's turned their marriage into some kind of joke."

"It's not just a joke! It's an agreement, Kethan! An arrangement made under pressure!" Priya's eyes sparkled with unshed tears. "They're not just two people in love. They're fulfilling a contract!"

Kethan stood abruptly, the chair scraping loudly against the polished floor. "A contract? You think that's all it is? How could he do this to her? To any of us?" His voice rose, echoing off the walls. "He promised me he'd treat her right!"

Priya crossed her arms, her stance firm. "Maybe he thought he could keep everything under control. But now, it's all unraveling. Ammu has no idea how fragile this really is."

Kethan ran a hand through his hair, frustration radiating off him. "I need to talk to him. Now."

As he stormed out of the office, Priya followed closely, her heart racing. They found Arhan in a conference room, surrounded by reports and a stack of paperwork. He looked up, his brow furrowing at the sight of them.

"What's going on?" Arhan asked, confusion painting his features.

Kethan didn't waste a second. "We need to talk. Now. You and I."

Arhan stood, an edge of defensiveness creeping into his tone. "What's this about? Can't it wait until after the meeting?"

"No, it can't!" Kethan snapped, his voice booming. "You've turned your marriage into a business agreement, Arhan! Have you even considered what this means for Ammu? For her happiness?"

Arhan's brows knitted together. "It's not like that. You don't understand—"

"Then help me understand!" Kethan shouted, the tension in the room thickening. "You're treating her like a pawn in your game. This isn't just some deal you can negotiate!"

Nishan, who had been leaning against the wall, raised his hands in mock surrender. "Hey, hey! Everyone calm down! We're all friends here, right?"

"Friends? Friends don't make a mockery of love!" Kethan barked, his voice dripping with venom. "You're supposed to protect her, Arhan!"

Arhan's expression hardened, and he took a step forward. "I didn't ask for this arrangement. It was done to satisfy our families. I thought we could make it work."

"Did you even think about Ammu's feelings?" Kethan shot back. "She's not some trophy to be displayed. She's a person, and you're treating her like a business transaction!"

Before Arhan could respond, the door swung open, and Hemanth, Ammu's father, stepped into the room. "What's going on here?"

The air thickened with tension, and Kethan's heart sank as he realized they were caught. "Uh, we were just discussing—"

Hemanth's eyes narrowed. "Discussing what? I heard you shouting about a marriage. Is my daughter's happiness on the line?"

Arhan stammered, "Mr. Hemanth, this is a misunderstanding. I—"

"Misunderstanding?" Hemanth interrupted, his voice low and simmering with anger. "You're married to my daughter, and I've heard whispers about this agreement. You think this is some kind of game?"

Kethan stepped forward, his voice steady. "Sir, we're just trying to make sure Ammu is okay. She deserves to know the truth."

"The truth?" Hemanth's face flushed with anger. "The truth is that my daughter deserves more than a conditional marriage! What kind of man are you, Arhan?"

Nishan shifted uncomfortably, his usual charm fading. "Look, maybe we can sit down and—"

"No!" Hemanth's voice boomed, cutting through the tension. "You won't sit down and discuss the terms of my daughter's life like it's some business deal."

Arhan's expression shifted, the bravado slipping away as he faced the reality of what his choices had wrought. "I never meant for it to be like this. I care about Ammu."

"Caring isn't enough when you've built your relationship on shaky ground," Hemanth shot back. "You need to fix this. Now."

Kethan exchanged a glance with Arhan, the weight of the situation settling in. They had to make things right, not just for themselves, but for Ammu, who deserved a marriage filled with love and trust, not just contracts and agreements.

"Let's talk," Arhan finally said, his voice softer, tinged with regret. "Let's fix this. For Ammu."

As they stood in the dim light of the conference room, the air was thick with unspoken words, and each man understood that the road ahead would be fraught with challenges, but it was a road they would need to walk together.

Chapter 21

Mr. Hemanth

The conference room felt suffocatingly small as the air crackled with tension. Hemanth stood with his arms crossed, a storm brewing in his eyes. Arhan felt the weight of his father-in-law's gaze, a mix of disappointment and anger swirling around him like a tempest. He glanced at Ammu, who stood beside him, her expression a mixture of confusion and fear.

"I can't believe you'd turn my daughter's life into a contract, Arhan," Hemanth said, his voice low and dangerous. "Ammu deserves better than this mockery of a marriage."

"Mr. Hemanth, please," Ammu interjected, her voice trembling. "We—"

"We love each other!" Arhan cut in, desperation creeping into his tone. "This was never just a business arrangement for me. Ammu means everything to me."

Hemanth's gaze didn't waver, his brows furrowed in disbelief. "You think saying that will change anything?

You've built your relationship on shaky ground. How can I trust that this isn't just a phase for you?"

Ammu's heart raced. "Daddy, please. I know it was arranged, but I love him. We can make this work!"

"Love?" Hemanth scoffed, shaking his head. "What do you know about love? You're just a child, playing house with a man who sees you as a business deal."

Arhan clenched his fists, frustration boiling beneath the surface. "I may not have asked for this arrangement, but I care for Ammu deeply. I want to make this marriage real."

"Then prove it," Hemanth shot back, his voice rising. "Prove you love her. Because right now, all I see is a man who's willing to walk away at the first sign of trouble."

Ammu's eyes welled with tears. "Daddy, please don't do this. I want to try! I believe in us!"

"You're mistaken if you think this is going to end well," Hemanth replied, his face hardening. "I've made my decision. You'll get a divorce."

The word hung heavy in the air, a finality that struck Arhan like a blow. "Mr. Hemanth, please—"

"No!" Hemanth thundered, cutting him off. "This is not up for discussion. I won't let my daughter suffer because of your foolishness."

Arhan's heart raced, panic setting in. "You can't just—"

"Watch me," Hemanth said, his voice cold as steel.

Ammu's hands shook, her heart breaking at the thought of losing the man she had just begun to love. "Daddy, please! You can't take him away from me!"

"It's for your own good, Ammu," Hemanth said, his voice softer now, but firm. "You need to understand that love isn't enough if it's built on a foundation of contracts."

Arhan felt a surge of determination. "If it's proof you want, then I'll give it to you." He turned to Ammu, desperation shining in his eyes. "Ammu, can I—"

"What are you doing?" Ammu's voice was barely a whisper.

Ignoring the disapproving glare from Hemanth, Arhan stepped closer, his heart racing in his chest. "I need to show your father that I'm serious about this."

"Arhan, wait—" Ammu began, but he silenced her with a finger on his lips. He leaned in, the world around them fading away as he captured her lips with his.

The kiss was electric, a spark that ignited the tension in the room. Ammu melted against him, her worries slipping away in that moment. She kissed him back, her heart racing, feeling the sincerity in his touch.

Time stood still as they lost themselves in each other, oblivious to the disapproving coughs and the shocked gasps from their families.

When they finally broke apart, Arhan's breath was heavy, his eyes searching Ammu's. "I love you," he said, his voice barely above a whisper, but loud enough for everyone to hear. "I'll fight for us. I won't let this end like this."

Hemanth's expression softened, but the resolve in his eyes remained. "A kiss doesn't change the reality of your situation. You still have a long way to go to earn my trust."

Arhan straightened, confidence flooding back into him. "Then I'll do whatever it takes. I won't give up on Ammu. I'll prove to you that I'm worthy of her heart."

"Words are just words, Arhan," Hemanth replied, his tone still firm. "Show me with your actions."

Ammu looked between her father and Arhan, her heart swelling with hope. "We can do this, Daddy. We can make it work. Just give us a chance."

The tension in the room was palpable as Hemanth's gaze flickered between the two of them. "Very well, but understand this: if you fail, I won't hesitate to pull my support." He turned, his voice steady. "You have one month."

As he left the room, Ammu turned to Arhan, her eyes shining with determination. "We can do this, right?"

Arhan nodded, his expression fierce. "Together. We'll show them what love really means."

With a shared glance filled with unspoken promises, they stepped into the future, ready to face whatever challenges awaited them.

Chapter 22

Arhan's Master Plan

The morning sun streamed through the tall windows of Arhan's penthouse, bathing the sleek, modern space in a warm glow. Arhan leaned against the kitchen counter, a steaming cup of coffee in hand, his mind racing with plans. He glanced at the calendar. One month. That's all he had to prove himself to Hemanth.

His phone buzzed, pulling him from his thoughts. Kethan, his ever-reliable brother and secretary, appeared on the screen.

"Arhan, have you thought about the trip to Manali?" Kethan asked, his voice steady. "It could be a good opportunity to smooth things over with Ammu's family."

Arhan nodded, biting his lip. "I want to impress Hemanth. Show him I'm serious about Ammu. A family trip should do it."

"Good idea. But remember, Hemanth has made it clear he doesn't want Ammu spending too much time with you."

"Let him try to stop us." A smirk spread across Arhan's face. "We'll just have to be clever about it."

The following week, the air in Manali was crisp, with snow-capped mountains towering majestically against a clear blue sky. Arhan stood by the fireplace in the lodge, his heart racing as he watched Ammu laugh with her sister Priya and Ananya, their laughter ringing like music through the cozy room.

"Are you sure this is a good idea?" Nishan, Arhan's best friend, leaned against the mantel, his playful grin betraying his skepticism. "Hemanth is right there."

"Hemanth doesn't know I'm planning to sneak Ammu away," Arhan replied, his eyes glimmering with mischief. "It'll be fine."

"Just remember, if you get caught, I'm not bailing you out," Nishan chuckled, raising his hands in mock surrender.

Arhan's gaze flickered to Ammu, her bright eyes sparkling as she caught his glance. She waved, her clumsiness evident as she almost knocked over a stack of mugs on the table.

"Careful!" Priya scolded, stifling a laugh.

Ammu grinned sheepishly, her cheeks flushed. "Oops! Sorry! I'm just too excited to be here!"

Later that evening, as the families gathered for dinner, Arhan's heart thudded against his chest. The atmosphere was lively, but the tension was palpable. Hemanth's stern gaze didn't leave Arhan for long, and Arhan fought the urge to fidget in his seat.

"Let's toast to family," Hemanth said, raising his glass. "May our bonds grow stronger."

Everyone echoed the sentiment, glasses clinking together, but Arhan felt the weight of Hemanth's scrutiny. He caught Ammu's eye across the table, and a spark ignited between them.

"Can we go for a walk later?" he mouthed, hoping she understood.

Ammu's eyes widened, a look of mischief crossing her face. She nodded subtly, her lips curving into a smile.

After dinner, Arhan excused himself from the table, claiming he needed some fresh air. He could feel Hemanth's piercing gaze on his back, but he pressed on, stepping outside into the cool night. The snow crunched beneath his boots as he paced, waiting for Ammu.

"Arhan!" Her whisper floated through the night, and he turned to see her slipping out of the lodge, a playful grin lighting up her face.

"Come here," he beckoned, his heart racing as she approached.

"What if my dad sees us?" Ammu asked, glancing over her shoulder nervously.

"I'll be quick." He took her hand, pulling her behind a large pine tree, the scent of fresh pine mingling with the chilly air.

Ammu's laughter bubbled up, and Arhan couldn't help but chuckle along. "You're so clumsy, but I love that about you."

"Stop it!" she giggled, her cheeks flushing. "You're making me blush."

"Good," he said, stepping closer, his eyes locked on hers. "I want to kiss you, but..."

"But what?" Ammu's voice was barely a whisper, filled with anticipation.

Arhan leaned in, his heart pounding. "But I don't want to get caught."

Before he could bridge the distance between them, a voice boomed from behind the tree. "Ammu!"

Both of them froze, panic flooding Arhan's veins. Hemanth stood there, arms crossed, his expression thunderous.

"What are you doing?" Hemanth's voice was low and dangerous.

"Daddy!" Ammu squeaked, stepping back as if she had been caught with her hand in the cookie jar.

Arhan straightened, his composure faltering. "Mr. Hemanth, I was just—"

"Just what?" Hemanth interrupted, his eyes narrowing. "Planning to sneak kisses while I'm right here?"

"Dad, we were just—" Ammu began, but Hemanth silenced her with a stern look.

"You're not to be alone with him again," Hemanth warned, his voice firm. "This is unacceptable."

Ammu's shoulders dropped, disappointment etched on her face. "But, Daddy—"

"No buts!" Hemanth turned, frustration evident in his stance. "We're leaving."

As he walked away, Ammu's eyes brimmed with tears. "I'm sorry, Arhan."

"Don't be. I'll find a way to make this work," he said, determination flooding through him. "I promise."

Ammu nodded, her expression shifting from despair to hope. "Together?"

"Always."

And with that, they both knew the fight had just begun.

Chapter 23

CEO on His Knees

The morning air in Mumbai felt heavy with an impending storm, but all Arhan could think about was the storm brewing in his heart. He paced outside Hemanth's office, his mind racing with thoughts of Ammu and the fleeting moments they had shared. He had never pleaded for anything in his life, but today was different. Today, he would fight for her.

With a deep breath, he pushed the door open, stepping into the room where Hemanth sat, his expression as stern as ever. Arhan's heart pounded, each beat echoing in his ears like a drumroll announcing a fateful confrontation.

"Mr. Hemanth," Arhan began, his voice steady despite the turmoil inside. "I need to talk to you."

Hemanth looked up, his eyes narrowing. "About what? I hope it's not about my daughter."

"It is," Arhan replied, stepping closer, his hands clenched at his sides. "I know you want to keep her away from me, but you have to understand—"

Hemanth raised an eyebrow, clearly unimpressed. "Understand what? That you want to steal my daughter away under my nose?"

"No, sir. I want to show you that I can make her happy," Arhan said, his voice softening. "Ammu has brought color into my black-and-white life. I've never felt this way about anyone before. She taught me what love really is."

"And you think that's enough?" Hemanth's voice was cold, but Arhan could see a flicker of doubt in his eyes.

"I'm not asking for much," he continued, desperation creeping into his tone. "Just a chance to prove myself. I promise I will never let her cry. Not as long as I live."

Arhan took a step forward. "Please, sir. I can't lose her. I'd do anything to keep her in my life."

The tension in the room thickened as Hemanth's expression shifted, contemplating Arhan's words. With a sudden rush of emotion, Arhan fell to his knees, grasping Hemanth's leg. "I'm begging you! Don't take her away from me!"

Hemanth's eyes widened in shock, a mixture of surprise and grudging respect in his gaze. "Get up, Arhan. This isn't how a CEO should act."

But Arhan remained on the floor, vulnerability spilling from him like water. "I don't care about being a CEO. I just care about her. Please give me one last chance."

A silence enveloped them, and Arhan could feel the weight of Hemanth's scrutiny. He held his breath, waiting for the verdict. Finally, Hemanth sighed, his shoulders relaxing slightly. "Fine. One last chance. But if I see you hurt her in any way, I won't hesitate to take her away. Understand?"

"Thank you!" Arhan exclaimed, relief flooding through him as he rose to his feet. He stepped forward, wrapping Hemanth in a firm embrace. "I won't let you down."

Ammu stood outside the office, her eyes wide as she witnessed the scene unfold. When Arhan emerged, he swept her into his arms, holding her tightly against him. "I'm so glad I fought for you, my clumsy princess."

Ammu giggled, relief washing over her. "I was so scared, Arhan. I thought I was going to lose you."

"Never. I'll always fight for you," he promised, his voice low and filled with conviction. They shared a moment, the world around them fading away as they embraced.

That night, the air was thick with anticipation as they found themselves alone in the glow of the dimly lit room. Arhan's heart raced as he looked at Ammu, her hair cascading over her shoulders, her eyes sparkling like stars.

"Ammu," he began, his voice husky, "there's something I need to ask you."

She tilted her head, curiosity etched on her features. "What is it?"

"Can we... um, take our relationship to the next level?" He swallowed hard, his cheeks warming. "I can't control myself anymore."

Ammu's eyes widened, a blush creeping up her cheeks. "But... I'm scared. What if it hurts?"

Arhan stepped closer, his expression softening. "I promise, I'll be gentle, my clumsy princess. I'll make it special for you."

Ammu bit her lip, weighing her thoughts. "You mean it?"

"Every word," he replied, reaching for her hand and intertwining their fingers. "You can trust me."

The hesitation in her eyes melted away, replaced by a glimmer of excitement. "Okay," she whispered, her heart racing in sync with his.

With a tenderness that belied his usual arrogance, Arhan leaned in and brushed his lips against hers, igniting a spark that set their worlds ablaze. Each kiss deepened their connection, pulling them closer into a whirlwind of passion and love.

In that moment, everything felt possible. Together, they were ready to embrace the next chapter of their lives, one filled with laughter, love, and uncharted territory.

Chapter 24

His Love for Her

The morning sun peeked through the curtains, casting a warm golden hue across the room. Arhan stirred slightly, the soft rustle of sheets drawing him from the depths of sleep. Beside him, Ammu was already awake, her heart fluttering with the thrill of the moment. She found herself enchanted by the sight of him—his dark hair tousled, his handsome features relaxed in slumber.

With a giggle that bubbled from her lips, she reached out, her fingers brushing through his hair, trailing down to his cheek. "I can't believe this is real," she whispered to herself, a smile spreading across her face.

As her fingers danced along his jawline, Arhan's eyes fluttered open. "Mmm," he murmured, blinking against the daylight. The moment he registered her presence, a grin broke across his face. "What are you doing, my clumsy princess?"

Before she could answer, he lunged at her, fingers wiggling as they found their way to her sides. "Tickle attack!" he declared, laughter spilling from his lips.

Ammu squealed, squirming away from his grasp, her laughter echoing like music in the room. "Arhan! No! Stop!" she gasped between giggles, her body writhing as he continued his playful assault.

"Never!" he replied, pinning her down with a triumphant grin. Their eyes locked for a moment, and the world outside faded into oblivion. Then, as if drawn by an unbreakable force, their lips met in a soft kiss, electric and tender.

When they finally pulled away, Ammu bit her lip, her cheeks flushed with happiness. "Are you going to the office today?" she asked, her voice hopeful.

"Anything for you, princess," Arhan replied, his thumb brushing against her cheek. The sincerity in his eyes made her heart race.

She beamed at him, a wave of joy washing over her. "You have no idea how happy that makes me! I've always dreamed of this—of romance, love, and a future together. It's like my life has turned into one of those dramas I used to watch!"

"Really?" Arhan chuckled, rolling onto his back and pulling her with him so she lay beside him, their bodies close. "I remember you used to get lost in those stories. What's the dream, huh?"

Ammu's gaze drifted to the ceiling, a dreamy look taking over her face. "Well, it was always about finding someone who would love me for who I am, clumsiness and all. I wanted grand gestures, heart-fluttering moments, and a love that felt like a fairytale."

Arhan turned to her, propping himself on one elbow. "And you think I'm your prince charming?"

"Absolutely!" she declared, her eyes sparkling. "But you know what? At first, I thought you hated me for being so clumsy."

He laughed, a deep, rich sound that resonated in the air. "I did, to be honest. You were a walking disaster. I couldn't understand how someone could trip over their own feet so often."

Her brow furrowed, mock offense taking over. "Hey! That's not fair. I've improved!"

"True," he conceded, a teasing smile playing on his lips. "But I love you for it now. You bring a lightness to my life that I never knew I needed. You're the sunshine of my life, Ammu."

Her heart swelled at his words, warmth flooding her chest. "I love you too, Arhan. Forever."

The sincerity in her voice wrapped around them like a blanket, and Arhan leaned in, capturing her lips in another kiss. This one was deeper, more passionate, filled with everything unspoken between them—the promise of a shared life, the certainty of love that had blossomed overnight.

As they pulled away, breathless, Ammu playfully poked his side. "So, what's the plan for today, Mr. CEO? Should we start planning our fairytale wedding?"

Arhan raised an eyebrow, a smirk creeping onto his face. "A wedding? Isn't that a bit premature? We just got married yesterday!"

"Details!" she exclaimed, rolling her eyes with a laugh. "Ammu and Arhan: The Clumsy CEO and His Princess. It sounds like the perfect rom-com."

"Clumsy CEO?" he repeated, feigning offense. "I'll have you know I run a million-dollar company!"

"And I'll have you know I trip over air!" she retorted playfully, causing both to burst into laughter.

"Okay, fair enough. But if we're planning a wedding, I expect it to be extravagant."

"Deal!" Ammu said, her excitement bubbling over. "But with lots of pink and fluffy things! And cake! Oh, the cake has to be huge!"

Arhan shook his head, still chuckling. "You're impossible."

"And you love me for it," she replied, winking.

"True," he admitted, pulling her closer. "I do. And I always will."

As they lay there, nestled in each other's warmth, the world outside continued to bustle with the rhythm of Mumbai, but in their cocoon of laughter and love, time stood still. With each passing moment, the bond between them grew stronger, weaving together the threads of their shared dreams into a tapestry of hope and joy.

Chapter 25

The Happy Ending

The sun dipped low over the Mumbai skyline, casting a warm golden hue across the bustling city. A year had flown by since Ammu and Arhan's whirlwind marriage, and the couple found themselves navigating the complexities of life together. Their apartment was a kaleidoscope of colors and chaos, a fitting reflection of Ammu's clumsiness and vibrant spirit.

Ammu stood by the window, staring out at the traffic below, her thoughts drifting. She picked up a plush toy from the couch, a gift from Ananya, and squeezed it. "I can't believe it's been a year, Mr. CEO. You still haven't let me touch your precious office," she teased, glancing over her shoulder at Arhan, who was engrossed in his laptop.

Arhan looked up, a smirk playing on his lips. "That's because you'd probably spill coffee on my reports. Or worse, take a selfie with my clients."

"Hey! That was one time!" Ammu protested, her eyes wide with mock indignation.

"Yeah, one time too many," he chuckled, closing the laptop and standing to join her. "But I wouldn't trade your chaos for anything. You make my life... interesting."

Ammu turned to him, her heart swelling. "Interesting? Is that your way of saying you love me?"

"Of course I love you," he replied, feigning exasperation. "Just don't remind me of my last quarterly report."

With a playful roll of her eyes, Ammu leaned against him, a content smile on her face. Just then, her hand slid to her stomach, a sudden pang shooting through her. She winced, biting her lip.

"Everything okay?" Arhan's tone shifted, concern etched on his features.

"Yeah, just a little... weird feeling," she said, trying to brush it off.

"Maybe it's the leftover pizza from last night," he teased.

"Or maybe it's a sign that I need more ice cream," she shot back, grinning.

Later that evening, Ammu and Ananya ventured out for a girls' day, laughter bubbling between them as they strolled through bustling streets lined with shops.

"Okay, spill," Ananya insisted, nudging Ammu with her elbow. "What's going on with you and Arhan? You two seem inseparable."

Ammu smiled, recalling the countless moments of joy and mischief they'd shared. "He's been amazing, honestly. I think he's finally starting to bend a little, you know? Like when he let me rearrange the living room and didn't even complain."

"Wow, that's monumental! But what about Vihaan? How's he holding up?" Ananya asked, her tone serious now.

"Better, I hope. He apologized after our last hangout. I think he just got caught up in his feelings," Ammu replied, her thoughts flickering to her childhood friend.

"Good. He needs to move on, or I'll have to set him up on a date with Kethan," Ananya said, smirking.

Ammu laughed, shaking her head. "No, please! I have to live with Kethan. I can't have him dating my best friend's ex."

As the sun began to set, they stopped by an ice cream stand. Ammu's eyes sparkled as she ordered a double scoop of chocolate fudge. "This is what I need! Ice cream cures everything, right?"

"Except you might need to share it with Arhan when he gets home," Ananya teased.

"Not a chance!" Ammu said, her mouth full of ice cream. "This is mine!"

The following week, Ammu felt the weird sensations growing more frequent. She decided to consult a doctor, dragging Ananya along for support. After a tense wait, the doctor revealed the news that would change everything. "You're pregnant, Ammu."

Ammu's heart raced. "Pregnant? Are you sure?"

"Absolutely," the doctor confirmed, smiling kindly.

"Oh my God!" Ammu gasped, her eyes wide. "Arhan is going to freak!"

"Let's tell him together! He'll be thrilled!" Ananya said, bouncing on her heels.

With a mix of excitement and nerves, Ammu called Arhan, her fingers trembling as she held the phone. "Arhan! Can you come home? I have something important to tell you."

"Is everything okay? I'm in the middle of a meeting," he replied, his voice laced with concern.

"Just... come home, please? It's urgent."

"Alright, I'll be there in thirty," he promised, his tone serious.

When Arhan stormed through the door, his expression shifted from worry to confusion as he took in the scene. Ammu stood in the living room, Ananya beside her, both of them glowing with excitement.

"What's going on?" he asked, looking between them.

Ammu took a deep breath. "I have a surprise for you!"

Before he could respond, she grabbed his hand and pulled him to the couch. "Sit. I've got something to show you."

"What is it?" He was visibly puzzled.

"Close your eyes," she instructed, her heart racing.

"Okay..." Arhan obliged, his brow furrowing.

Ammu fished out a small onesie from a bag resting nearby. "Open!"

His eyes flew open, and confusion morphed into realization. "Is this... a baby onesie?"

"Yes!" she squealed, unable to contain her joy. "We're having a baby!"

For a moment, silence filled the room. Arhan stood frozen, his mouth agape. Then, suddenly, he swept Ammu off her feet, lifting her into the air. "Oh my God! Are you serious?"

"Yes! I'm serious!" she laughed, wrapping her arms around his neck as he twirled her around.

"Wait, wait!" He put her down, his eyes shining. "You're really pregnant?"

"Yep! And you're going to be a dad!"

He pulled her close, his voice thick with emotion. "You have no idea how happy this makes me. I mean, I knew I loved you, but this—"

"Arhan, you're scaring me. Are you okay?" Ammu teased, a laugh bubbling up.

"I'm more than okay! I'm—" He abruptly stopped, then grinned. "I'm going to be a dad! Our little princess is on the way!"

Months passed, each day filled with Arhan's unwavering support and love. He doted on Ammu, ensuring she ate properly, walked regularly, and stayed as happy as possible. Their home was filled with laughter and anticipation as family and friends rallied around them.

Kethan and Priya were ecstatic when they learned the news. "Ammu, I can't believe you're going to be a mom!" Priya exclaimed, her eyes sparkling.

"Does this mean I get to spoil my niece?" Kethan chimed in, a grin plastered on his face.

"Absolutely! As long as you don't let her play with your gadgets," Ammu warned, crossing her arms playfully.

The day of reckoning arrived, and Ammu was filled with a mix of excitement and apprehension. Arhan held her hand tightly in the delivery room, his eyes never leaving her face.

"You're doing amazing, Ammu. Just breathe," he urged, his tone soothing.

"Easy for you to say," she gasped between contractions, squeezing his hand. "You're not the one pushing out a watermelon!"

"Okay, fair point," he chuckled nervously, wiping the sweat from her brow.

Hours felt like days, but finally, the cries of a newborn filled the air. Ammu and Arhan exchanged a stunned glance, emotions swirling in their eyes.

"Is it a girl?" Ammu asked, her heart pounding.

"Yes! A beautiful baby girl!" the doctor announced, handing the tiny bundle to Ammu.

As she cradled their daughter for the first time, tears streamed down Ammu's cheeks. "Look at her, Arhan. She's perfect."

Arhan knelt beside her, his heart swelling with love. "She's ours. I can't believe we created this miracle."

"Who do you love more?" Ammu teased, her eyes sparkling with mischief even through her tears.

"Seriously?" he chuckled, leaning in closer. "You know you're my number one, Ammu. Always."

Ammu smiled, a wave of warmth washing over her. "And you're my number one too, Arhan. I love you."

As they exchanged glances of love and admiration, the world outside faded away. In that moment, they were a family, bound by love and laughter, ready to face whatever came next together.

And as they began their new journey as parents, one thing was clear: love was the greatest adventure of all.

Acknowledgements

To my wonderful parents—thank you for your unwavering support, love, and belief in me. Your encouragement has been my foundation, and without you, this journey would not have been possible. Every word I write is a reflection of the strength and values you've instilled in me.

A heartfelt thank you to my dear friends Arun, Sai Lakshmi, Sanjay. Your patience, insight, and dedication mean the world to me. Reading my novel not once, not twice, but multiple times just to help me make it better is a kindness I will never forget. Your feedback, encouragement, and unwavering faith in my story have shaped it into what it is today.

I am profoundly grateful to my faculty R.Ganesan Sir. Your belief in my abilities ignited the spark that set me on this path. Your support was the first step of my journey, and it continues to inspire me every day.

I am endlessly grateful to have you all in my life. This book is as much yours as it is mine.